PHANTOM

By
Dan Hart

to Cheryl & Jerry
good friends. Thanks for
being you. Dan Hart

Note for Librarians: a cataloguing record for this book that includes Dewey Decimal Classification and US Library of Congress numbers is available from the Library and Archives of Canada. The complete cataloguing record can be obtained from their online database at:
www.collectionscanada.ca/amicus/index-e.html
ISBN 1-4120-3861-8
Printed in Victoria, BC, Canada

TRAFFORD

Offices in Canada, USA, Ireland, UK and Spain

This book was published *on-demand* in cooperation with Trafford Publishing. On-demand publishing is a unique process and service of making a book available for retail sale to the public taking advantage of on-demand manufacturing and Internet marketing. On-demand publishing includes promotions, retail sales, manufacturing, order fulfilment, accounting and collecting royalties on behalf of the author.

Book sales for North America and international:
Trafford Publishing, 6E–2333 Government St.,
Victoria, BC V8T 4P4 CANADA
phone 250 383 6864 (toll-free 1 888 232 4444)
fax 250 383 6804; email to orders@trafford.com

Book sales in Europe:
Trafford Publishing (UK) Ltd., Enterprise House, Wistaston Road Business Centre,
Wistaston Road, Crewe, Cheshire CW2 7RP UNITED KINGDOM
phone 01270 251 396 (local rate 0845 230 9601)
facsimile 01270 254 983; orders.uk@trafford.com

Order online at:
www.trafford.com/robots/04-1669.html

10 9 8 7 6 5 4 3 2 1

Phantom. Something apparently seen, heard or sensed, but having no physical reality, ghost, specter. 2. An image that appears only in the mind. Unreal; ghostlike.

PHANTOM

Places of operations: Philippines, Japan, Taiwan, Korea, Singapore, Australia, Viet Nam, Laos and Cambodia.

Primary function: To track down and return to U.S Military base, Embassy, Consulate or U.S. Ship any deserters, AWOL'S or just plain stupid individuals who failed to return or think there in love.

Talents: Ability to fit in anywhere, bribe locals, knowledge of vessels, weapons, self defense and flat survival under any conditions, inability to stay out of trouble.

Escalation of activities: Talents needed in Laos, Viet Nam and Cambodia. Schooled in Languages at Foreign Service school Washington D.C.

Subject name: Jack O'Brian, age: 34 yrs. ht: 5'10", wt 182, eyes: hazel hair dark brown, build wiry, expert karate, Kubota, rifle, pistol, Pacific Fleet boxing champion 1950,51,52, trained diver, air force survival school Panama, Philippines, field trained Marine Base Quantico, Va. Small vessel operator, trained Little Creek, Va. considered an Irishman with an attitude.

How the hell did I let myself be talked into this goddamn two year tour of duty in the Navy, that's why I'm here seeing you Doctor, I know now that I'm crazy.

How did it happen? This from the Navy psychiatrist.

One day in the small town in Idaho where I'm bartending in walks the ugliest most misshapen individual you've ever seen in your life, which also happens to be an old shipmate of mine and is now the Navy recruiter for the area. We got to talking about our days at Sub school in New London, Connecticut, our first diesel boat and the times we had in the Atlantic and Caribbean. Next I know he's giving me the pitch about a new two year program for guys like me, re-enlist, give it a try for a couple of years, don't like it your out. Damned if it didn't sound good. Say two years real fast and its nothing, now that I'm back in uniform it seems like an eternity.

You're far from crazy sailor, do your tour and enjoy, if you still feel the same later, get out. As I headed for the door he said, nice try!

There's a lot to be said for discipline, for the other guy anyway. Eating, working and sleeping regularly were a shock to my system. Being older then the average sailor awaiting assignment, the Bos'un in charge of the outgoing units put me in charge of morning and afternoon muster. That was it, my one and only duty, then I was set to hit the beach for the rest of the day.

When uniforms were issued, after several days of testing and medicals, this is when I ran into my first problem in this mans new Navy. In the Old Navy, I had a regular uniform, pullover jumpers and bell bottom pants with thirteen buttons. The supply department looked as though it was taken over by Filipinos.

When I refused the button shirts and the pants with zippers and threatened to kick the pygmies ass if he didn't quit fooling with me, the duty Warrant Officer walked in. He heard the commotion from his office in the rear of the warehouse. He asked the questions, I answered. He had his crew issue me the old style uniform, and then gave them hell for keeping the old style uniform for their special buddies. The only request made by the Warrant was, that I make myself scarce, he made it very clear what would happen to me should I enter his Supply area again.

While awaiting assignment as an engineman anywhere I received a call to report to the Chief Master at Arms of the base. What now. Master Chief Oates was one big dude and old Navy with no time for bullshit. Without preamble he said, "O'Brian I've been sent your service jacket from the Provost Marshals Office. Seems during your last tour with us you had a knack for problem solving when you weren't creating them, you've been assigned to me temporarily. I'll give you whatever you need to do the job if it's within my power. According to your record anything you've ever needed in the past you seemed to appropriate through whatever means, do your job and do me a favor, don't get caught. This is Thursday, report to me Monday morning in civvies, dismissed."

Imagine three days running loose in San Francisco, heaven help me (or them.)

Monday at 0730 I was at the MA shack slightly hung-over but ready to go out into the world and punish the miscreants violating rules of the Navy, (Uniform Code of Military Justice).

The Chief walked in handed me a folder, "In the folder O'Brian you'll find names of some of our finest who have decided they like the beach better then the base, get your ass out there and find them and bring them back, there's vouchers in the folder for expenses, not beer money sailor."

When a sailor disappears look no further then the nearest pub then for the bar maids, sailors are either horny or thirsty, don't look in church for them.

First name on the list, Hiram Mohammad, Oakland address. Shit, not my lucky day. Down on Seventh Avenue in Oakland across from the main post office is a group of bars, a liquor store, and a sidewalk with door-to-door pimps, hustlers and prostitutes, not a welcoming place for an Irish honky.

Walking into Ethel's is a real experience. All white eyes and teeth; fortunately one can't see the frowns and unwelcoming scowls. The bartender was huge and as bald as a cue ball, but I wasn't about to comment on it. I ordered a bottle of Bud, sat at the end of the bar and let my eyes adjust to the dim interior. Lo and behold who is cozied up at the back table with one of Oakland's finest but my missing sailor Hiram. Calling the bartender over and explaining to him my purpose for being in his fine bar and further explaining that I had to call for a pick up for the errant sailor so I wouldn't bother the local fuzz who were waiting outside, a clumsy lie that could have cost me my teeth. Must be my lucky day, he said get the freeloader out of his joint, he's out of money, bumming drinks and hustling his girls and they got to spend time with the money customer, and he ended with "thank you". He gave me his phone to boot.

When I called the chief he thought I was full of it, I'd only been gone an hour. He showed up in less then twenty minutes, Hiram was no problem due to his condition, which was washrag limber. He'd been gone AWOL for two weeks. This is good for a couple of weeks in the navy brig, to give one time to assess the meaning of responsibility and the warning imposed.

No thanks, no job well done, this is the Navy, get your ass in gear and quit goofing off, get it on.

The next two names on the list were buddies who hung out in a joint up on Powell, they had been running loose (AWOL) for a week and were about to miss their orders to a vessel which would put them in a world of shit. Missing ships movement is serious and you could sit in the brig a long time waiting for the ship to return stateside, six to eight months.

That afternoon and the next morning I hung out at the Hot Nut, or out on the street, and was starting to get some suspicious looks from the regulars in the area, not to mention I was starting to get a buzz on from the drinks I'd had while waiting.

After dinner I returned to the bar, the off going barmaid pointed me out to the bouncer, he wasn't bashful when he asked me what the fuck I wanted hanging around his joint.

My mistake, I told him, who said the ass was well padded and could take punishment, bullshit I hurt now thinking about the foot he put in my ass.

Being a glutton for punishment, the next afternoon I took up station outside the Hot Nut again. After being refused service inside I returned outside only to be rewarded with the appearance of a cab discharging the objects of my search. Two grubby teenage out of uniform bombed out of their skulls, seaman. Words were spoken. I ID'ed myself and placed them under arrest. Then the shit hit the fan. The bouncer came out and sundayed me, knocked me into the two sailors. One banged his head against the cab, and went out like a light. The other I elbowed in the balls on the way down. I bounced off the pavement and kicked out behind me, got the big bastard in the solar plexus, he went down I got up. He just made the wrong move on an Irishman. After I bruised my knuckles on his ugly face, I returned the favor and put a foot in his ass. I commandeered the cab. After cuffing the two punch drunk AWOL's and drove straight to the base, where they were taken into custody to be held for orders to their ship, or just hang around the brig until their ship returns from operations. Well the chief did warn me that this wouldn't be a walk in the park.

Next day true to form, the Chief chewed my ass for not calling for backup and charging the cab. He did however voucher four of his biggest staff to go to the Hot Nut and read out of the good book chapter and verse to the bouncer, one of life's small rewards.

Knowing every time you go out you could get the shit kicked out of you has you practicing humility and a false hope that there really is a thing to the story of a guardian angel looking out after you.

My next month had me hither, thither and yon. Goddamn Chief handed me every shit detail the others couldn't or hadn't been able to handle. I became real intimate with the Bay area and surrounding environs, especially the dumps and dives and their patrons, who were one step away from the streets, and harboring those unfulfilled dreams and fantasies.

It was these same people that were responsible for my success, they had my number at the base and kept me informed who was where and when, the price of a cheap bottle of muscatel or an even worse tasting pint of cheap booze was their reward. Once in a while I'd spring for a small buffet setup of cold cuts and salad, hell you'd think I was the male version of Mother Theresa.

The payoff was beyond the Chief's expectations. He still grumped about the outlay anyway, even though I was responsible for better then thirty missing men returned to duty and through the efforts of my posse of barroom talent, four deserters turned themselves in to me. The Chief got all kinds of recognition for a job well done and he chewed my ass for creating extra work for his department. When my orders came through, you can bet your ass he didn't have tears in his eyes.

Taipei

What the hell was the Navy thinking? What the hell was I going to do in Taipei? My orders were for the Nationalist Army Barracks in downtown Taipei, I remember them being behind the National hotel downtown and a very expensive watering hole. No amount of nosing around gave me any insight as to what my new assignment was to be.

Surprise, surprise, Taiwan is one lovely Island but I wasn't there to sight see, shit!

Made no sense for the Army (theirs not ours) to send a limo to pick up an enlisted man with three red stripes on his jumper and one hash mark. That's right, just a damn fireman.
Don't ask, I had more time up and down in rate then an escalator in a department store. Lack of respect for authority had something to do with it.

I was delivered to a small building that was to be my living quarters. I was met at the front door by this little gnome of a man who immediately took possession of my sea bag and disappeared into the interior of the building, where upon entering I found all my uniforms dumped on the floor, not one of my happiest moments. My houseboy was taking charge and this was the start of his project to have my uniforms cleaned, pressed or washed whatever. Surprisingly his payoff or reward however you look at it, was to be my can of shoe polish. I could live with that, this was how he earned his extra money, shining shoes on the base.

My houseboy, I was soon to discover, was a fount of information, great knowledge of the Island and worth a case of shoe polish.

By the time I'd settled in, the Navy liaison office, manned by one lone Navy Chief, was closed for the night. Being a typical sailor I headed for the bright lights of Taipei, naturally.

At the front gate, I was met by a guard who was carrying a weapon bigger then he was. Closer inspection showed it to be a B.A.R. For the uninitiated that's a Browning Automatic Rifle, the weight alone is enough to give a husky man a hernia, that's why there's always a two man team operating it. The M-60 is more to my liking and doesn't spray the world like the browning.

Small base, he knew who I was, or at least knew I belonged there, The Sergeant of the guard insisted I join him for tea at the NCO mess before I went ashore. When in Rome. His purpose or intent was to show me where to eat while on the base and the chow hall never closed, wages are nothing, so they could afford to keep the rice bowl full twenty four hours a day, some of the help worked just for the left over food to feed their families.

After hanging around long enough so as not to hurt anyone's feelings, or be the cause of anyone to lose face, I headed for the bright lights and a cold beer.

Wearing civvies fools no one on a small island. No sooner had I hit the streets then the hustling started, rich American right, wrong. I was damn near broke after my flight and hadn't hit the disbursing office as of yet.

Lounging against his cab in front of the National Hotel was my answer to information please, there's always a part of any town no matter where the locals play and the price is right, a quart of beer is about forty-nine cents American opposed to the going rate of Three dollars American in the hotels and tourist traps.

After turning down the offer of a cab ride due to low finances, the cabbie couldn't believe anyone especially an American was that broke or for that matter that cheap. Out of curiosity rather then generosity he convinced me the ride was free and he took me to his sister's bar, away from the beaten path.

This is something I don't recommend for the light of heart, the unsuspecting or the loner. Strange town, stranger customs and very poor people make for explosive situations, especially when you have no idea about local attitudes toward Caucasians, let alone Americans.

This is one of those times where I was lucky instead of foolhardy. Turned out Soo Wang, the driver, was bored and was quitting for the evening anyway. We arrived at the club of his sister after about a twenty minute drive, what a treat, the club was on the side of a hill overlooking the Tamsui river and had one hell of a view down the canyon.

Soo introduced me to his sister and some of his friends and ordered us a couple of beers, known as Tiger Piss. The sister, Son Soo offered us noodles when we settled in a booth, Soo ate like he hadn't eaten in a month, the more he liked it the louder he slurped. Hell, everyone could hear him over the music. The evening progressed nicely. I was introduced to what seemed like a million people all with Chinese names and unpronounceable to boot. I refused more beer due to my current state of poverty and was ready to return to the base, this was not to be the case. A night out to these people meant just that, night out.

Sometimes my attitude shines through as cocksure and confident, no one gave me any hassle or tried to hustle me, don't ask me what we talked about but we found some common ground, and had one hell of a nice time.

Six AM came real early and as I walked through the Base Gate, salute and all, I knew there would be hell to pay later with jet lag and being up all night.

After a shave and shower and fighting off the gnome of a houseboy, whose name was Chin and thought it was his job to dress me as well as keep up my uniforms and billet, he ranted and raved about my all night sojourn and his worry about my well being. I really think his main worry was I wouldn't be around to get him more shoe polish. Jesus I didn't need another Mother.

The NCO mess decks adopted me as there own, by the time I got through shaking hands and bowing I was ready for another beer to settle my nerves.

There's something about rice and fish heads for breakfast that is unsettling, Barfh. Custom calls for the guest to have first choice out of the pot and as stated, fish heads are a delicacy in that part of the world. This is one time I put the old Irish charm to work and tried to be as diplomatic as hell. It worked. Amen to that brother otherwise the previous evenings merrymaking would have been all over the mess decks.

When I reported to the chief in the morning, he said, "Now there's two navy men here, I know what I'm doing here but no one else seems to know what your doing here, or what your function is to be, any ideas O'Brian?"

"Not a clue chief, orders will catch up with me I'm sure, in the meantime chief I'm broke."

"Sorry O'Brian, my office has no funds for that, any monies will have to come from the Air Force paymaster. Talk to him, in the meantime stay out of trouble and my way. I've nothing for you to do; if and when your orders show up I'll get in touch with you. That's all, enjoy the island."

The Air Force disbursing office was next door to the Navy office, which simplified things. Any service man who has traveled on orders has found out the hard way that you do not leave base without your pay records on your person, any Government entity can pay you as long as you have your records. As it turned out I had three weeks pay coming plus travel pay and per diem. Damn, I was rich; the rate of exchange was almost fifty-to-one. When I left the disbursing office I was three feet off of the ground, bring on the good times.
Talk about a kid in the candy store, Taipei is one gorgeous place. The rainy season, June through August, had just ended and it seemed everyone had spring fever. I've never been a tourist with a planned itinerary. I started walking let things happen naturally. Chung Shan N. Road led me to the railroad station where I grabbed the train. The view was something to behold, everything fresh and green. I got off at the Government Tourist Bureau and walked back towards the center of town on Chung Hsiao E. Road. By the time I arrived at the Lai Sheraton Hotel I was one thirsty pup. Cheap bastard that I am, I almost cried when I got the bill for the two beers. Even with the exchange rate I knew the Sheraton would not be one of my haunts, back to going native.

At this point I grabbed a cab back to China Town. Small Town atmosphere, the cabby asked if I was Soo Wang's friend. No secrets in Taipei. The driver and I had lunch at his cousins restaurant. Again I met people with unpronounceable names and lots of them. I was invited back for a wedding the following week. This gives great face to the parents of the bride to have a visitor from America at the wedding. After finagling an invite for my buddy Soo I went searching for him. Not too tough, there he was leaning on his cab thinking of quitting for the day. The other cabby and I explained where I've been all day and it wouldn't do but we, the three of us had to return to his sister's bar to plan for the next weekend wedding.

As luck would have it, three Air Force pukes, or was that punks, came in looking for trouble. After slams of gook lover, chink lover and one too many middle fingers, I decided it was time for me to improve inter-service relations. After all, there were only three of them, small too. Barroom brawls are no time to ask the rules or give warning of intent. Its called getting it on, get it over with and return to your drinking, or whatever sport you happen to be involved in at the time.

The action was over as soon as it started, with minimal damage to the bar. The police came out of the woodwork. As I earlier stated, everyone on the island is related and this gathering was no exception. The rabble rousers were returned to base and my friends and I, with a couple of off duty police returned to the task at hand, which was seeing how much beer we could put away.

The next few days were the same. One ran into the other, meeting my new friends and seeing the sights. We attended wrestling, kick boxing, hell, we even went to the Confucian Temple. My circle of friends was rapidly expanding. Walking down the street you'd think I was running for Mayor or Governor of the Island.

The barroom fight was over as far as I was concerned, not so the Air Force. Someone hurt their people and therefore must pay. That's if they could prove who it was, and that's when I was called on the carpet. Seems the description of the thug who whooped up on several of the Air Force pussies fit me to a tee.

The Chief was unhappy, especially since he didn't know who or what I was or what I was supposed to do while on the island. The Air Force Lieutenant was doubly pissed because he knew less then the Chief. The messages started flying. Who the hell is Jack O'Brian and where are his orders? No one came forward to positively ID me as the culprit who physically assaulted fellow servicemen. You can bet your ass they knew.

The coming weekend was the Chinese wedding bash, so my Chinese friends and I got together and paid for the honeymoon trip to Tainan on the south coast of Taipei, but not before we lost a day at the wedding, these people really know how to throw a party. Having been accepted into their group of friends and relatives was to serve me well during the rest of my stay on the island.

Next day was a Monday. Such a hangover, I should wish on my worst enemy. The call came to report to the Chief at the office. My orders were hand delivered, unusual, try unheard of. The Chief had company when I arrived at the office, two big mothers, American, and in civvies. First impression is, "Augh shit, what now." The Chief was excused and the Navy NIS, Naval Intelligence Service, began the rundown on what was expected of me, not only on the island but the rest of Asia during the rest of my tour. Sounded like the end of my thoughts of fun and frolic.

Seems temptation for the troops coming into the port of Kaohsiung, (Cowshung) is out of control. Most of the girls are Eurasian, Chinese and white Russian mostly and flat beautiful. They are known as the girls without a country. Ineligible for passports as non-citizens, they enter into the only profession open to them, that's right, Hotel hostesses. The sailors think they're in love and want to spend the rest of their life nestled up to these beauties. Only when the money is gone so is the girl who only a couple of days before swore her undying love. I love you. No shit, buy me a drink. Standard form of introduction in most bars in Asia.

Kingdom hotel overlooking the harbor and located for convenient access by the Navy and Merchant Marine ships that enter the harbor seemed to be the biggest problem. Although well run, clean and has Chinese decor with one hell of a fine restaurant there wasn't much management could do about the girls. They were a way of life and brought the sailors in, according to the apes from NIS.

I was to go to Kaohsiung, check into the hotel and feel my way from there. My primary function would be to see that no lovers remain in the hotel at departure time. That included all personnel either civilian or navy. Man would that prove a rough order, Fortunately the local police would be my backup. They would be effective only because they hated the paper work these malingerers created for them and fining broke sailors reaps no rewards, they already spent all their money.

The party started all over again that night when Soo Wang found out about my departure. I packed before leaving the base, which proved to be fortuitous. I was leaving from Sung Shan Domestic Airport on a Mac flight the next A.M. at 0945, (Military Air Command) run by the military, piloted by civilians, after a night of drinking with all my new friends in Taipei and I felt like I had a drink with each and every one of them. I was delivered to the airport by a procession that made the wedding party look very small by comparison. A few eyebrows were raised, but nothing said. That's one plane ride I could have done without. Wow, was my stomach doing flip-flops and I was a color of green St. Patrick would have envied.

Kaohguing

The airstrip was just that, a strip used mostly for the military as a cargo shuttle. Again the looks started. Who the hell is that guy and how does he rate a flight? If they had asked me, I'd have opted for the bus.

My thoughts on the plane ride were simple, I'd proven an embarrassment to the powers to be and they just wanted me the hell out of their hair, that's O.K., they didn't impress me either.

Lo and behold, who the hell should meet me, but another damn Wang. Soo must have been on the phone to his relatives, as much as I wanted a get-well beer, the thought of another group of drinkers was not on my agenda.

Fortunately this member of the Wang family was of a serious nature. A family man and unlike my friend Soo, had to make a living. He drove me to the Kingdom Hotel, which sat right on the river. After signing in at the desk Sun Yat, Soo's brother, saw me to my room. Shit monks had more space then I had. Sun Yat went through the roof and started spouting off in Chinese to the porter. Back to the desk, more jabbering bullshit which was not setting well with my hangover, the short of it is, I was put in a room facing the river on the second deck, believe me this was luxurious compared to the first room.

The NIS was sparing no expense to see to my creature comforts, bullshit, you can bet your ass they were well put up, as a matter of fact they never left the comforts of Taipei, and damn I have no great love for those freeloading bastards.

My work was cut out for me that's for sure. That afternoon my favorite bureaucrats showed up with my work agenda, I've read thinner dictionaries, they had fourteen files, the latest being six weeks old, they either thought I was a miracle worker, or this was their way of telling me my attitude was not appreciated. Years later I was to run into one of them on Guam. He was a GS (Government Service) seven, not very impressive after all those years of service; he had to be a screw-up. As for myself I was a GS twelve, believe me it didn't take me long to rub his nose in it.

My friendship with the Wang clan was to pay remarkable dividends. The wedding I attended in Taipei was another godsend; the father of the bride was the leader of the Hong Kong Green Tong for the island of Taipei, If you have to have friends. That night after the puppets left, I took in the local color at the bar of the Kingdom. I'll tell anyone here and now the beauty of the Eurasian is not exaggerated, these ladies in their tong sons with the split clear up to their tush was enough to make the local missionaries forget their preaching.

The place was jammed with merchant sailors, and not an American in sight, not to get nervous you say, evidently you have not traveled the world, Americans are not to well accepted. I used to say I was Irish or Canadian, learned that the hard way in Hong Kong years earlier after some limy sailor decided he wanted to change my looks, better known as rearrange my features. Damn near got the job done but the army sent down a group of peacekeepers from up on the hill, better known as Victoria Barracks. I went through the men's room, over the wall into the adjoining junkyard where I had to run for my life from the biggest damn dog you've ever seen. Big bastard didn't speak English, but that's another story for another time.

At the end of the bar I observed the activities without staring at anyone, and enjoyed a nice cold Singapore Steam beer only because they didn't have Black Swan. The bartender called me by name, Mr. O'Brian, doesn't ask, I figured he was somehow related to the Wang's.

Next morning bright and early, I was ready to perform my primary function, after coffee. Shops in the hotel closed; out on the town to find my coffee, nothing. Closed up tighter then a drum, hell it's the crack of dawn. About five A.M. I wandered down to the ships tied up for unloading of cargo, as a sailor I know the ships have coffee round the clock.

The gangway watch was asleep, and not too happy to see me, he directed me to the mess decks anyway. This was no problem, as I hold a license in the Merchant Marine as a staff officer (Purser) and a regular "Z" card that every Merchant Mariner carries. The cook fed me and was tickled to death to have a visitor that early in the morning, he was a Kiwi, New Zealander to you, and on the return trip leg of there journey of about four months.

We visited for a while then I went back to the hotel to start work, if you can call it that.

Message at the desk was the phone number of the cab company should I need any transportation during my stay. You've got to love these Chinese, so gracious yet vicious when crossed, or made to lose face, as would be the case if I did not take them up on the offer of the cab. You see, the company was owned by the Green Tong and I was a friend of the family. If I wanted, I could have given my file folder of missing sailors to the tong and sat at the hotel bar and awaited the results, in fact that's damn near what happened.

Being an early riser was unusual for visitors in this part of Taipei, noon is more to the liking of the late night partiers. Coffee was served to me on the dining room terrace, though that dining room didn't open for several more hours. My floor boy heard me in the shower and alerted the kitchen staff, his position is service and security, though I can't prove it, I'm sure he deals in gossip and information.

My third morning I had visitors; in they walked looking very officious and all business. The lead man slight of build, in uniform, had to be one tough puppy. He had enough gold on his uniform to have been a general. Nothing quite so grand, he was the local brigadier of police and his associate built like they were twins, was in a suit that was west in cut, and no way he bought it on a chief inspectors salary. I offered them a seat; we had coffee and talked about the weather. It's considered rude to get down to business right away, as most of us Westerners are prone to do, bad for the digestion.

The purpose of the visit was to offer assistance of their departments should the need arise, immediately I jumped on the offer and asked for assistance of the immigration people as well.

US personnel I could voucher to the nearest US base in the company of marine guards, pulled off of embassy duty for just that purpose. The local police would hold US citizens until transport could be provided, and I would see that the police received compensation for room and board. We're not talking about the Hilton here. Foreign personnel caught up in the sweep would be deported to their closest embassies or Consulate's.

It should be noted that any personnel wishing to return to the Island, had to go through channels to immigrate. They didn't know that by remaining in the country and entering illegally by jumping ship, their chances of returning were nil, period, and the loss of their sailing papers was also a forgone conclusion. The only way to return would be to swim or row a boat. Even then the individual was faced with prison time for illegal entry, then barred from ever returning. To me, this is a real shame, the people are so gracious, and the climate can't be beat. It's a man's dream come true.

After ironing out the details guess who shows up, right, the bureaucratic dinks from NIS. Their bowing and kowtowing was enough to make me lose my breakfast, let alone face.

I'm used to working as a group of one and playing it by ear, here these two clowns want a play by play rundown of what I was up to and my plan of attack. Being my lovable sweet self I told them to flat fuck off, Christ what a couple of idiots.

You can bet your sweet bippie that they were on the horn to whoever is responsible for incompetents in Asia, and the message traffic, my name and attitude outstanding, I'll just bet the wires were burning up.

They were finally appeased by the Admiral from CincPac Headquarters, (Commander in Chief/Pacific), in Subic Bay, Philippines. He offered to keep them posted as to my activities and extracted a promise from them that they would stay out of my hair, of course the Admiral was on the phone to me at the hotel, when you hear on the phone an aid say, hold for the Admiral, you know enough to give your soul to Jesus because your ass belongs to the Admiral and you are in what is commonly referred to a world of shit.

This is all new to me, only because up until this point I had no idea who I was working for, well that got cleared up in a hurry, believe me.

I was warned that after shitting in everyone's mess kit I'd damn well better show some results and justify my attitude, or I would find my new quarters at Portsmouth, N.H. (Prison) uncomfortable. What an attention getter.

That afternoon I started cruising the streets of Kaohsiung with my trusty guide and driver Kip Ying who played tilt with the car due to his bulk and it wasn't fat either, he knew every joint in the city as well as every person. I swear, he was allotted to me for that purpose, I'm sure, plus the benefit of protection should that need ever arise. We visited some dumps that made the Bowery in New York look like Fifth Avenue.

The number of Caucasians was mind-boggling. Hell, it looked like I'd be here the rest of my life chasing down deserters and ship jumpers, aw shit, and I've been in worse places.

There's no way, once you've heard it, can you mistake a New England or New York accent. One you can't understand, the other grates on your nerves. As luck would have it we ran into three of the boys from the same ship out of New York, only thing, the ship sailed a couple of week previously. After buying them a drink and getting the low down, I had Kip call the locals for a pickup. These guys were so broke, it wouldn't have been long before they would have gotten into trouble rolling a cab driver or one of the ladies of the evening. No I don't feel like a louse, I probably saved their lives; they would have been killed on the street, or in the local lockup.

Human rights are not a big priority with the Chinese.
Enough for one day, Kip returned me to the hotel, and told me to be ready for dinner by ten P.M. that night. These people call that a civilized time for eating and starting the night. What was I going to say, no? Remember who he works for and where I was getting all this cooperation from. I retired to the bar for a couple to unwind, ran into my favorite people (NIS) made my

report verbally, promised a written report next day and went to my room to nap.

The floor boy already knew I was going out, what time, and who was picking me up. Mr. Yip Pin Sin my benefactor and host was prompt, and believe me when I say I wasn't about to keep him waiting, I was right at the door to the hotel, never even stopped for a drink at the bar.

We went to the Shanghai restaurant. Guess who owns it. I thought those places were only in the movies, what a beautiful décor. We were greeted like visiting royalty and seated by a huge window with a view that was to kill for. The menu was mostly seafood dishes with rich, somewhat salty sauces. "Drunken" chicken, bean curd pork, Ningpo-style fried eel, West lake fish, green cabbage hearts with dried mushrooms, and shark fin soup, this was one meal to remember. The company was pleasant but I knew better then to get carried away and impressed with myself, in the back of my head was the ever present thought, behave yourself.

We had an after dinner brandy, I was asked if my accommodations were satisfactory and was I getting the cooperation I wanted from the locals. If I wanted for anything I had but to ask.

The limo dropped me off at the hotel and I was beat. The service people at the hotel did everything but carry me to my room, they knew who I was having dinner with that evening. Man I could get used to this life. They even had a couple of Singapore Steam beers on ice for me, did I die and go to heaven or what.

The blinking red light for messages was on, the Chief Inspector for the local police would be picking me up at 0530, that's A.M. for a workout at his dojo before starting the day's routine.

I thought I was in shape until I finished my hour's workout with the Inspector. To say he kicked the hell out of me would be an understatement, he hit and kicked me hard and often and hardly worked up a sweat, I swear he had a secret smile on his face. After the workout we had a light snack, discussed business and it was quite clear that he'd already done research on my project, had the manpower in line and knew where the bodies were. He returned me to the hotel to change, gave me an hour before he would be back to pick me up and we could start our roundup.

The next week was hectic to say the least; the NIS was jumping for joy at the end of every day and was no longer skeptical where my previous successes were concerned.

The message traffic was considerable; the Admiral received his reports, as did Yip Pin Sin up in Taiwan.

My ever-present peace of mind came from the presence of Kip Ying, the King Kong look alike who was my guardian and protector, and on more then one occasion he pulled my bacon out of the fire. There was the time we were going into a real dump of a hotel, the police were in front of me on the second floor, the clowns we wanted were on the first floor visiting the ladies, here I am between the police, and two very pissed off merchant sailors who liked their life on the island and had no intention of returning to the good old US of A, at least not without a small punch out.

They had me cornered and got a few licks in (that hurt) before man mountain dean picked them up by the neck and shook them, he wasn't an easy man to get through to, his job was to see that no harm befell me, to him that meant removing any and all threats permanently, and these clowns were starting to work me over pretty good. Hell I thought I could hit hard. He released them to the police, reluctantly I might add, he returned me to my hotel for the evening, damn did I need a drink.

By this time everyone in the place knew who I was and what I was doing. For some of the girls this was the answer to a problem, namely the sailor or in a couple of cases airmen, who were broke and no longer could afford the girls. They were happy to see them go and turned them in, their reward was fresh meat (new sailors with money) that were pouring into the harbor in record numbers due to the conflict in Viet Nam.

My stay came to an abrupt end, at least sooner then I expected, my success rate far surpassed the original folder and the Admiral had other fish for me to fry. I made many friends on the island, and was comfortable there, tough shit, to quote the Admiral.

My new orders would be sent down to me within the week. A Navy tanker headed for Viet Nam would transport me to my next duty station, which was to be with the Navy advisors group out of Hue and just below the 17th parallel, (better known as SOG, Special Operations Group) shit, looking on the map they might as well have sent me to Hanoi, I was damn close, and this did not leave me with a great sense of well-being.

Just Below the 17th Parallel

Finally I finished my assignment on Taiwan, was through taking crap from the clowns with NIS, now it was time for a little R&R.

In all fairness to the people from NIS, in my experience's with them all over the world, they are a group set apart, and I truly believe they, as a group, couldn't find the water if they fell out of a boat.

The word was out about my departure and the parties started. At first I thought that they were just happy to finally be rid of me, then I realized I had really made some fast friends and lasting friendships.

The hotel decorated the dining room, the people from Taipei started showing up, what a treat to see old friends. Soo Wang along with his sister and the rest of his cabby buddies. Hell surprise of surprises, Yip Pin Sin and his entourage showed up with a fan fare you had to witness to believe.

We had a nice visit in his suite shortly after his arrival, I had nothing but praise as to the way I was treated and especially for my shadow Kip Ying, boy did that Kip beam, how's that for face. We had two glorious days of food, drinks and flat hell rising, boy was I going to miss these people.

The oil tanker had by this time arrived in Port, my orders arrived the day before and I'd had them for three days now, I was to report aboard for berthing and transport, immediately. Yeah sure, they could live without me for a few days, after the way I'd been living you have a life size picture of me settling for a crowded berthing space with the accent on smelly feet, bad breath, body odor, and watch changes every four hours, so shoot me.

The Kingdom hotel was a popular watering hole for the tanker crew, so I got to watch some of them in action, no different then any other sailors I've seen the past month.

The curious glances were there as no one had seen me before, and not in uniform, I was treated well by the hotel staff, which really aroused the curiosity of a few of the officers from the tanker.

A few of the guys from engineering I met I asked about the ship, they were non-committal; they had been briefed about talking to strangers.

Three days in port and fuel replenished, the vessel was ready to go. I was driven dockside by Kip Ying and reported aboard in uniform, a lowly fireman. The executive officer was notified, had me brought to his quarters and commenced to chew me a new ass. It seems I was three days late in reporting. I reminded him I was there for berthing and transport only, so how the hell could I be late, again the attitude showed through and got me an interview with the Captain.

He was a no shitter but had sense enough to see my logic, just a warning to steer clear of the exec.

He called sickbay for the chief corpsman to make arrangements for a bunk. Amen, no smelly berthing with the crew.

An hour later as lines were cast off, the clamor from dockside was something to hear. I was unpacking my sea bag up on the 02 level in sickbay and went out to see what was going on, I swear half of Kaosiung was on the pier yelling goodbye, no doubt organized by Mr. Green Tong himself.

Again I was not the execs. favorite person, I was beginning to think I would have to give him swimming lessons before our next destination.

My first order of business was boots for the jungle, and fatigues, no way was I going to run around Viet Nam looking like one of a kind. The supply department acted like I was speaking Chinese, funny they were all Filipino, their were so many of them on this ship I wondered what damn Navy I was in, they're still not my favorite people to serve with.

My request through the exec., you guessed it, denied. You can imagine my surprise when a seaman with a striker badge of radioman, struts down the deck one morning in full regalia of the man in combat, jungle boots, fatigues and the saltiest damn combat hat you've ever seen. I wasn't ships company, permanently assigned, so I had no clout.

The Captain soon had an earful, as did the supply officer. What the hell were they going to do, throw me out of the Navy? Don't throw me in that brier patch. The exec. was soon searching me out and decided I had too much time on my hands. Guess who ended up being the ship's mess decks master at arms, sort of a waiter captain with muscle, that's right, yours truly.

Ensign Dickhead had the duty for mess decks cleanliness and quality of the food, this is a riot, most of these clowns thought shit wrapped in cellophane was a holiday treat, he and I hit it off immediately, it was hate at first sight.

The report he wrote had the old man on the mess decks the next day to see this mess for himself, I told him the kid was an asshole and shouldn't be out in public without his mother, that didn't go over too well, especially coming from an enlisted man, the Captain gave the place a 4.0 it doesn't get any better then that, baby Ensign was relieved of any duties associated with the food service.

My next project given to me by the Exec. was integration, more togetherness for the blacks and whites. I argued that off duty they could damn well eat and talk with anyone they damn well please, it's been my experience that the black man would rather be with his own group, convince the exec. of that.
Boy did the shit hit the fan. In the chow line, I went around and said, black, white, black, white, the grumbling was worthy of any Navy man. I did the same thing on the mess decks, no tables full of whites or blacks only, now that was something to hear. I damn near had a full-blown riot on my hands. After the Captain got wind of this fiasco the exec. was told to steer clear of the chow hall and cut me some slack, shit guess who was always laying in wait for me, this cruise was not turning out to be my favorite thing to do.

I wondered why I never saw any of the Filipino crew on the mess decks. Low and behold the light was lit and I was shown the way. The bastards were getting special treats from the flip cooks out the back hatch of the chow hall, the Chiefs mess and the officers wardroom, one hand washes the other, they had their own little world onboard that ship. Again my popularity soared when I put a stop to that bullshit, it was, eat with the crew or go hungry, if they issued air I would have died from lack of.

Due to the increased activities of the Viet Cong up on the 17th parallel new orders came for me, the Captain was to drop me off at the mouth of the Mekong Delta below Saigon-Cholon area where the swift boats would effect a transfer at sea. I still hadn't been able to convince anyone of my need for some uniforms, after blowing the whistle on the flips my chances of cooperation from the supply department were next to nil, so much for Navy brotherhood.

It took the ship about another three weeks before we were to be at our destination, what took so long? The old bucket did an amazing eleven knots an hour, that's with the boilers full out, half the crew pulling the other half pushing. This created problems for aircraft carriers, in order to launch aircraft during refueling they had to maintain an average speed of approximately: fourteen knots.

The ship was the oldest tanker in the fleet held together worse then an old model "T" with chewing gum and bailing wire, but it was the most dependable in the fleet.

The crew had a sense of humor, one time when the carrier, The Constellation, was alongside the crew rolled out on the well deck butcher paper, which had written on it, "Fuck You." The duty Admiral failed to see the humor in this and requested the Captain send over the responsible party or parties. Request denied, we needed all our personnel.

The word came down from above like the voice of Moses, 'knock off the shit'.

The "Old Man" talked like a true sailor. The exec. on the other hand should have stayed in the seminary, straight laced New Englander if you ever saw one, pompous as hell and always in a snit. Shit it's a wonder his blood pressure let him live that long.

One time on the bridge, where I used to hang out when off duty, our gyrocompass went out. The quartermaster (steering person) helmsman to the initiated was given hell for not maintaining course, his reply to the Officer of the Deck was, the fucking gyro went out again. Wrong reply. He was told to get off the bridge and that he was on the report for his language. Just then the Captain stuck his head out of his sea cabin and said, " What's wrong, did that fucking gyro go out again", the Officer of the deck immediately told the quartermaster to belay that last order and to return to the wheel. It's kind of hard to chew ass when the Captain talks just like the enlisted men.

It wasn't long after this incident that we damn near went down from a collision with an LST we were refueling, again the damn gyro had screwed up. That rust bucket tanker had plates as thin as rice paper, Christ they couldn't scrape paint off the hull for fear of punching a hole in her side.

Fire is one of the worst fears a sailor has next to colliding with some big bastard that's going to chew you up and spit you out, and from the way the Captain of the other vessel was yelling and carrying on I can't help but feel he too felt strongly about being smacked in mid ocean. Some people just fail to see the humor in most situations. He lost the lifelines and rafts on his starboard side and we suffered minor damage on our portside including one lifeboat station and our lifelines, fortunately that was the extent of our topside damage. The question was did we suffer any below the water line.

My personnel jacket was in the possession of the Captain and was restricted and confidential for his eyes only, I guess they felt he should at least know who he was transporting. The exec. was always curious but that came under the heading of tough shit, he was out of the loop on the need to know basis, any time he was pissed made my day.

This was mentioned only to make you aware that the Captain knew that I was a diver as stated in my record, and guess who he called to go over the side to assess the damage to the hull.

When the gear was brought up from the boson's locker I was to use to dive, I damn near had a heart attack. Shit, I've seen better equipment being used in a kiddie wading pool, this didn't cut any ice with the old man, and over the side I went. That rust bucket piece of shit was so covered with barnacles its a wonder I wasn't cut to ribbons below the water line. I inspected the outer hull for damage while the damage control people conducted their investigation internally, as far as opening and inspecting all voids on the port side aft, void is just what it sounds like, a space surrounding the ship to eliminate the possibility of taking on water from a collision without any safeguard, picture it as inner wear and outer wear as in a diver suit.

When sailing along on any ship, due to trash and garbage being thrown over the side, the ocean scavengers better known as sharks follow along. After a half hour in the water it seemed they were taking an inordinate interest in the tasty morsel dangling in the water, namely me, enough already. Believe me the hull wasn't damaged.

You'd think that out of a crew of fifteen officers, thirteen chief petty officers and two hundred and fourteen enlisted, one swinging dick would have had some training in diving, wrong. I firmly believe after being on board with these people for three weeks that to them duty was a dirty word, they weren't all losers, I'll bet out of the whole lot maybe fifty-four were salvageable.

My parting shot was one of my nastier ideas in some time, part of the engineering crew was involved with the repair of all auxiliary equipment, motor launches, ships cars, of which they carried two, deck winches and the laundry.

One of the new ensigns decided that the "A" gang crew could no longer have access to the laundry for personal use, if your to fix it you should know how it works, right, wrong. According to the logic of another dickhead ensign, you need steam to operate the laundry, my suggestion was merely to go to the fire room, (boiler room) and remove the main steam valve to the laundry for overdue maintenance, this happened to be officers wash day, what an attention getter, didn't take long for the shit to hit the fan.

Three days later the supply officer who happened to be a lieutenant up through the ranks, got the drift and pulled the order, returning laundry privileges to the men of "A" gang, the laundry was operational within thirty minutes, amazing.

Vung Tau

Word came down from the powers that are for me to get my ass in gear and be ready to move within twelve hours, I was to be picked up by the swift boats for transport to my next haven, which happened to be below Saigon on the delta, a place called Vung Tau. I'm packed and ready to move out when the boats are picked up on the radar about fifteen miles out, next there spotted coming over the horizon twenty minutes later, busting water and out running a squall, the sea had risen a bit and gave us some whitecaps to contend with, nothing we couldn't manage.

With the first pass of the first swift boat my sea bag was given the float test, second pass it was retrieved, me next, although in good shape I still ended up in a heap on the stern of that damn swift boat, as quick as they came, we were gone.

How the fuck do you justify running open water in Indian country to pick up a piece of shit enlisted, who the hell is that good, me, that's who.

I've taken my share of shit from RMEF's (rear echelon muther fuckers), I want on a picnic, shit, I'm as old as the average Admiral, only I've had a hell of a lot more experience.

Hell, we had a run of about forty minutes before we hit base. No one said hello, or welcome aboard, fuck, what the hell was I the duty leper.

Month later I was to find out that was just the way I was described to the group, mean, trained full of hate and vicious. Shit, draw your own conclusions.

When I was dropped off at what was referred to as headquarters, put me in the presence of a goddamm lieutenant of the United States Navy, a real class act from the US of A Annapolis. Shit, I was ready to give those assholes some walking room, eliminate the old bastard from the fucking melee.

Nothing I enjoy more then a goddamm good fight, even if I had to travel half way around the world to find it. I don't deal well with fucking amateurs, but I didn't sign on to commit suicide.

Better known as the skipper, this young prick had the respect of his crew and that is what separates the men from the boys. This guy had hair on his ass and balls bigger then the Philadelphia Liberty Bell. The man's name was Mulligan; spelled with a capitol Donald, graduate of that phony school on the hill known as Notre Dame.

My introduction was, get your ass in gear and get aboard that boat, leave your gear, if we don't make it back you won't need it anyway.

The outward run consisted of checking all weapons and firing burst to be sure everything is in working order. Ever shoot a 81MM with a 50 mm hanging on, praise be to the man looking over me, hell yes, god, I'm good with both. The 81 is a mortar that is cocked like lever action Winchester, sight down the fifty sights on top and pull the trigger, effective as hell and accurate as well.

Just let me give you some idea of the weaponry on these small swift boats.

Over the wheel house is one 81 mm mortar, usually with a fifty mounted on top, twin Machine guns Port and Starboard, main engines are two geared diesels GM with 960 ship: 2 shafts and cut the water at about 28 knots.

The crew consists of one Officer and 5 enlisted, in my time in the area, I don't remember one person kowtowing to another, and this was a live or dies situation. All hands did their best to stay alive and protect their shipmates.

Running up on two sampans full of pleading people to be merciful was not a pleasant experience, two yelling for help, three preparing to throw grenades and four ready to strafe your ass, don't show your face Jane Fonda, or, is that Hanoi Jane.

Being my first experience of this kind I waited to follow the lead of the boat captain, in this case a first class boson's mate, when he gave the order to put hands over your head and turn around, the bow gunner laid a stitch of fifty fire along the side into the water. Let me explain this action, should he run the shot across the bow he's away from the action on board the sampan and it only takes seconds to bring weapons to bear and we could have been dog meat, it was obvious that no one was going to make a move. The next order was to sink them, the fifty cut loose again and hit them at the waterline, serious time, the group on the boat started grabbing weapons, too late, the firing from our boat increased and put an end to the farce.

We threw a phosphorus grenade into the middle of the boat and ran like hell up stream before one hell of an explosion rocked us and rained debris and body parts down from above.
These people were shipping explosives down for the sappers that hug the perimeter of all US installations; these people infiltrate areas at night plant their charges, set the fuse and crawl back into their hole.

Already a good day's work for this crew.

This trip was to give me an idea of what the swift boats did on the river, and that it was no glamour job.

On return to base I was assigned to the hooch with the crew of lucky thirteen, the fellers I had just made the excursion with. This lasted about two weeks before I started to draw complaints as to my personal hygiene.

In preparing for my stint into Cambodia, I stopped showering and bathed in the river only, the cong wasn't known for having an over abundance of soap, and eating rice balls with some fish mixed up in the mess, so my body odor would resemble that of the Vietnamese, or close I hoped.

Still no uniforms to be spared so I settled for some cotton pajamas, black the color of the cong uniform. Non-rustling type for silent skimming of jungle, no boots either so I went around wearing thongs, shower shoes. During my preparations no locals were allowed into or close to the base area, my presence was to remain as close to a secret as possible, this pissed off a few people who had become used to the Viet doing all of there work for next to nothing.

The skipper called me one morning, wouldn't let me into his hooch and had me stand downwind, does that tell you anything. He informed me that as long as he had been on the base message traffic has been minimal from headquarters, since my arrival the traffic has better then tripled but nothing for him, mostly me, he was not a happy camper.

He handed me a package from Headquarters. In the Philippines, it was the radio I had requested, the size of a Walkman with a dish antenna about the size of a coffee saucer with fifty feet of extremely lightweight connecting cable thinner then a hair. This radio was set to the CIA's satellite dish that flew over the area every twenty-four hours, and could penetrate rain and cloud cover. It had a small readout screen for message traffic, and one send button for location in which to keep track of me.

The package also contained the set of throwing knives I had requested in a vest type garment with twelve pockets. The knives were of a new lightweight material called titanium, and did not clink if hit together, practice with them was of interest to the group at the base, but all request for lessons in the art had to be refused, time for me was about up, time to move out.

The satellite mentioned earlier had spotted what it thought were a couple of Navy pilots being used as beast of burden close to the Cambodian border by local farmers. My job was to infiltrate the area and ascertain whether or not the photos were on the money, if so I was to report, wait for backup and lead the rescue group in to the area. I was given explicit instructions to stay out of harms way, follow orders and leave my initiative back at the base, yeah, sure.

If they thought so much of me, how come I'm going into Indian country alone and naked, (Naked, no backup or weapons), except of course my knives. I'd been going around smelling pretty ripe for a few weeks now; it was time to get this show on the road.

The morning of departure was giving us some favorable weather, real shitty with a real monsoon and low clouds; the order was given the night before, so there was no farewell committee.

Strange, we took off from Vung Tau headed across the bay and upriver to My Tho and then a straight run to Chau Doc, it took us about four hours of busting ass to get there, but these guys didn't want to be that far up river alone. My destination was a small spot called Takeo, smack on the border of Cambodia and Vietnam. I was unceremoniously dropped in the water at the rivers edge and damn near cut in half when the boat did an about face and hauled ass out of there.

Well here I was, my ass was soaked, I was in unfamiliar territory, all I had to worry about was the Cong, unfriendly locals, leeches and the green death, snakes that fall from trees for the purpose of killing something to eat. I understand the lapsed time from bite to death is a grand total of six seconds, should have brought an umbrella.

Well, I had about eight miles as the crow flies to my destination, it was coming on to noon, I hit the water and started wading, this was not going to be my fastest time for river travel that's for sure. Best I could do was keep my eyes open and expect traffic on Asia's highway, easier then walking.

After three hours in the water and feeling I'd donated enough of my life's blood to the leeches, I hid on the bank in the brush and put mud packs on the little dears, and smothered the shit out of them until they fell off, had no salt, didn't dare light a piece of punk I had for the purpose, so the old native remedy had to do.

Heard them before I saw them, floating down river as if on an outing came a small launch with six of the unfriendliness, talking and eating and ignoring their, I'm sure, orders to look out for the bogy man, that's me. Well now I know that the Cong is definitely about, I'd best pay attention to what the hell I'm doing, giving them time to get out of sight I scampered into the jungle and waited for dark, although I'm a sneaky bastard, I'm not invisible.

After the mud dried and fell off, taking the leeches with it, I climbed the nearest tree to check my surroundings. On the other side of the river I could see smoke curling up through the trees, how nice, a picnic in progress, fat chance, when in doubt stay put.

Night was a long time in coming, little activity on the river, the launch I'd seen earlier had returned and pulled in across the river where I'd seen the smoke. I heard splashing from the same area, which means to me that the Cong is taking a little R&R. There was no mention of activity in this area from the group that operates the spy satellite covering that area, evidently the cong had just infiltrated the area, and if it wasn't for bad luck I wouldn't have any at all. Shit, nothing to do but wait out the daylight and see what the evening brings. Five hours in a tree is enough to make you want to chatter like a monkey, your acting like one why not make noises like one, because you aren't ready to die that's why.

Two hours into darkness was quiet enough for me to decide to move out, keeping in mind that sentries could be and probably were posted on both sides of the river, best I could hope for was they had strung nothing across the river, such as cans to rattle or grenades attached to a trip wire. First thing you learn is never think your enemy is stupid, they have schools too, and they've been fighting a hell of a lot longer in their country, know the terrain and look like they belong there.

The return to the river and the leeches left me with one hell of a chill but it sure beat walking through the jungle where I'm sure Charlie was waiting.

After three hours of wading upstream I came out of the trees into a clearing. Sure this was my location, all I needed now was a place to lay-up and scope out the area in the daylight and see if the people I was looking for were in fact on hand.

A small stand of bamboo on a knoll behind some sheds on the edge of the field gave me a clear field of vision, anyone moving about would be easily seen in daylight. Dawn came and I was being eaten alive by the small bugs who thought my nose, mouth, ears and eyes were nesting places, tough, movement in this area would be spotted immediately therefore scratching and waving of hands in definitely out.

When does the guy sleep you ask, how about now, I'm human not superman, and even I screw up. When I opened my eyes the field had three guys working, and two guys behind them driving them on to greater levels of labor, one had a bamboo switch lambasting the shit out of two while the third one had a machete and was using the flat side to smack the third one to greater endeavor. The clown with the machete, from the looks of this one guys back, misjudged from time to time and he had a few lacerations visible from my viewpoint, which was at least a football field length away.

I'd come looking for two navy pilots, what's with three guys, from their size it was fairly obvious that they weren't slopes. This treatment went on most of the morning. Midmorning a truck came down the edge of the field, three men in civilian cloths got out walked out to the three people in the field, and relieved them of their prisoners, these three got into the truck and drove off. The beatings renewed with a passion from the fresh people now in charge. Shit and damn, I was told two, now I've got three plus six guards, this is turning into a real clusterfuck, if I wasn't so stubborn I'd haul ass on out of there. Some got three, some got nine, screw you buddy, I've got mine, if I did accept that attitude I'd never be able to hold up my head again. Besides, as I've always told myself, the reason for my attitude is I have no one that will miss me, not for as long as it takes to drink a toast to me, later the only person to miss me was my banker, I was screwing up his accounting and he didn't know where to send my savings or to whom.

The more these little bastards whomped on their prisoners, the stronger my resolve to see them released became. The three were roped together neck and waist and had water buffalo yokes strapped over their shoulders, this couldn't have been very pleasant, horseshit, you try it.

The work in progress brought the group closer to my hiding hole with every turn of the field, the guards had a habit of taking a break every half hour or so, two at a time leaving only one guard in charge for a period of about ten minutes. The odds of me taking out three at one time would not make the tables at Vegas, they were too great, then again the other three could return at any time. The time factor weighed heavily on me not knowing the area, when these guys might be brought back to camp for ongoing transport to another location as P.O.W.s, I felt like I was between a rock and a hard place, some decision.

The guards broke for lunch and hustled the prisoners over to the side of the field where they gave them some rice and some water. Damned if they weren't within spitting distance, any chance of communicating would shock the shit out of them and they'd react without thinking and then the doo-doo would really hit the fan, so I waited to see what would happen.

These guys hadn't been around long enough as prisoners to be run down and helpless, if I make my move I won't have to carry anyone, at last, something in my favor.

The guards were real lazy bastards, one fell asleep right now, one went into the woods, probably to bird watch, yeah sure, and the third dumb shit felt like kicking around the prisoners. Wrong move, now I was pissed, who said I was a reasonable man. The first knife went to the sleeper, the second caught the sadist beater, I lay in wait for the third, he didn't disappoint me. This all happened so fast it took the pilots a minute to grasp what was happening. I told them to remain seated where they were in case the other three drove up. They'd still have to cross the field to relieve Larry, Moe and Curly who have recently gone to the big Ho Che Min trail in the sky, this would give us an advantage of surprise. No way was I going to gamble on their return, it was inevitable, the only question was how soon. I had visions of us clearing the area and a few minutes later the alarm is sounded, our chances were slim to none should that happen.

The two pilots I was to pick up were one Lt. Commander and his weapons officer. Correction, two pilots I was to locate. They were from the Carrier the Constellation, the other hot-dog pilot was from the Carrier Ranger, and was only a guest here for three days, seems they were scheduled for transfer out the next day. Someone was really going to be pissed.

We worked out a plan to take the returning guards by surprise; again, no way can I handle three coming at me at once. As the sun hit the horizon, gorgeous sunset, the noise of the kerosene burning Junker was heard, here goes the adrenaline. Laughs and giggles accompanied the trio as they walked over the field. We had arranged the dead guards around as though they were still on alert, the guard in the lead must have been a bird watcher too for he walked straight into the wood without so much as a by your leave, the other two were a bit slow on the uptake before they realized things weren't as they should be. Too late, they were thrown down and muzzled just as the other guard came out of the toolies. Too late, the knife took him through the juggler; with no compunction the other two were dispatched to join Buddha in nirvana.

Close as we were to the river, we had no use for the truck, we drove it to the waters edge and let it go, we were right behind it. An hour downstream I sent up the balloon and gave it a three-time poke for emergency pickup, the Commander started giving orders before I told him to just enjoy the ride and shut the fuck up, told him to write me up later but if he interfered with me in any way in the course of my evasion I'd kill him, period.

Tough talk, hardly, we all wanted out alive and this is what I do, so let me do my job.

Around dark we came upon the campsite of the cong I'd seen on my way upriver, still no security on the river, maybe they know something I don't know, keep alert.

No visible guards, slack bastards, I motioned the Officers down stream and had them wait with instructions should I get in deep kemchi keep moving, the swift boat will show up before long.

Swimming to the launch tied to a tree, I sliced the mooring line and drifted with the boat down river. No alarms, hell I expected all hell to break loose, well I knew we weren't out of the woods yet. The group had kept moving down a short way and were having their first experience with the ever loving and hungry leeches, bitch, bitch, bitch, here we are swimming in warm water in a tropical paradise with a knowledgeable guide interested only in their welfare, piss on them if that's their attitude, I won't invite them back.

We clambered over the side after another half mile, picked up the oars and gave it all we had until we were out of earshot of the Cong we stole the boat from, then it was Katy bar the door, we went for all we were worth and what the engine could handle and hauled ass out of there.

We were, by now and my estimation, out of Cambodia and into Viet Nam, when the swift boats came upon us you would have thought we were just out on a picnic and floating down stream at our leisure. The Commander was still smarting under the rebuke he'd received from me, a lowly enlisted man, fuck him, I wouldn't tell him how to fly his plane, my mission, my decisions, hell, he could have stayed in Cambodia for all I gave a shit, he didn't waste a minute writing his report when we were returned to base, hero hell, I was an insubordinate piece of shit.

The sad part of this attitude concerning me seemed to be overall, all the explanations could not erase the fact that I had disobeyed orders, locate and report location, no more, no less. The fact that these guys were getting their ass kicked had no bearing on my decision, typical military snafu, enlisted men do not, repeat, do not make decisions, the REMF's do that even though none of them ever got far enough away from the Officers Club to need a shoeshine, this was all bullshit and I put that in my report and told the Admiral, not asked, to kiss my Irish ass, and relieve me of this assignment where I had to deal with candy assed pukes with no nuts and all mouth.

The reply was short in coming and to the point, stay and work as we had planned or return to Subic Bay in the PI and pick up my ticket for Leavenworth (US Navy Prison in New Hampshire) and prepare for a long stay. That folks is what is known as blackmail in the civilian world, orders in the Navy.

All the skills and training given cannot take the place of common sense and luck, nor can they replace ones sense of honor.

The taking of another humans life whether enemy or not, goes against the grain of all were taught throughout life, as in the case of this last encounter its you or them, and the latter is preferable to the alternative, however the picture stays with you of your actions and could drive you over the wall if you cannot put it, and keep it in perspective, no one comes away from these encounters untainted and unscathed.

The Navy Lieutenant in charge of the swift boats of squadron 13 called me in and said I was to have seventy two hours in Saigon before my next assignment up in Laos, I was lucky on my last infiltration, I knew the next time I was too far from the water to run and hide, the lieutenant took this opportunity to tell me what a royal pain in the ass I was and how I'd disrupted his smooth operation (his description, not mine) with my fuck it attitude and how some of his men have adopted same. I took this opportunity to tell the looie that he is a royal asshole and brown noser, and the best he could do was have me thrown in the brig, relieved of all duties and explain to the CinPac in Subic, his reasoning, then maybe I'd get lucky and they'd throw me out of the Navy, Here come that brier patch.

He said he'd settle for a punch out, well, if you insist, son of a bitch chickened out when he figured out that I wasn't going too, some shit about bringing himself to my level, hell that would make him almost a man, not quite.

Saigon

You'll never guess who I ran into at the base ops In Saigon, that's right, Commander wonderful himself, things are looking up, he turned red, then blue, then started in on what a disgrace I was to the uniform and I should be taken out and shot before I could father anymore like me. I was very polite, told him he was living proof that monkeys cross bred with Officers and with all due respect, please go fuck yourself, Sir: This word covers a multitude of sins and omission of navel courtesy.

The three officers I'd come down river with were on a flight out to the carrier Ranger, from there they'd be shuttled off to R&R (rest & recreation) a trip home, a fistful of medals and a good chance of advancement in rank, another group advancing to there level of incompetence, typical navy, a college education does not a leader of men make.

After my debriefing, I was escorted to the enlisted barracks, the duty yeoman promptly assigned me a bunk and a duty section which I just as promptly told him where to shove his duty roster, I'm in Saigon for rest and recreation only and all I require is a damn bunk. The shit hit the fan, he called the duty Chief who chewed on my ass for awhile, before I'd had it, and told him what I thought of his parents and their unwed status, that's the closest I've ever come to seeing another human explode.

Being unwelcome, I found the marine barracks and begged a bunk from them, they heard of me as being one crazy son of a bitch for the stunt I'd just pulled and were ready to make me one of their own. Naturally as fellow warriors they had to welcome me in the standard form, right, we went to town and got blotto to the eyeballs; we were in such bad shape we couldn't even get into trouble.

Next morning we paid the price with magnificent hangovers. The problem of men going AWOL (absent without leave) is not just a stateside problem, the Aussies call it gone on a walkabout, still means the same, your off the roster and some one has to pull your duty, this doesn't endear you to the crew, good way to get your ass kicked royally.

The duty marine gunny Sergeant was talking at breakfast about the problem, to show my appreciation for their hospitality, I volunteered to help search out the local environs for those missing from duty, some have seen so much that they've gone beyond the thousand yard stare and are flat dinky dau, spaced out and couldn't care less, in some case's drugs play a big part, drugs were a problem in Viet Nam, but not to the extent that some of the brass has reported.

Hung-over and sick I went uptown looking for some hair of the dog and scope out the local bistros. The streets were teeming with venders, women and military uniforms of all stripe, this I was to understand later is around the clock action nonstop, what a zoo.

Sightseeing has never been my forte, so I checked out a few of the gin mills off the beaten track, found one close to being clean and not much traffic and no girl-sans to bug the hell out of you to buy them a drink, their usual speech was, I love you no shit, buy me a drink, pretty romantic stuff wot, guess where they got their English lessons.

Mama-san was half articulate and was more then helpful when she found out I was looking for some AWOL's in my spare time. I explained there would be no trouble for the clowns who remained away they were just wanted back. No problem, she dispatched three of her girls and within an hour I was joined by three of the sorriest looking marines I'd ever laid eyes on. The same old story, broke, hung-over and had come to that realization, no money no love, they wanted a drink, a meal and a bed, the thought of returning to barracks had them scared shitless. On that count I was able to convince them of no court martial, however they would receive extra duty and suffer the wrath of their gunny Sergeant, whom I'd called incidentally to bring a truck and have the medics standing by with delousing materials. Pretty safe bet these guys had more then lice on them, they probably bent the pipes every time they took a leak.

After the gunny picked up his wayward boys and put them through the outstanding ass chewing that only a marine of that caliber can deliver, he had them stand down until the medics gave them a clean bill of health. These were three lucky marines, had their unit gone upcountry while they were gone, they could have been facing desertion charges, in time of war that's the death penalty.

Under the old Rocks and Shoals that governed military behavior, that would have been a very distinct possibility, under the new UCMJ, Uniform Code of Military Justice, discipline has hit a new low. When you sign on the dotted line instead of following without question, the new breed of enlistee, not all mind you, wimp and whine and go see the Chaplain about being picked on. This is basically the problem that faces the old gung ho fighting man, follow without question and rely on training received, every man is part of a well oiled team and every member has a job to perform, the safety of one and all depends on discipline and unity. These fellows at the marine barracks in Saigon were one close-knit unit.

During my three days in Saigon life around me became a bit cloudy, the gunny and I became fast friends and drinking buddies, we were both members of the old school where the military is concerned and conducted ourselves accordingly.

Although we were both avid beer lovers we refused to drink local beer or booze, local stuff was rumored to have from time to time, ground glass or bamboo inserted for your discomfort, like punctured intestines and a fast case of bleeding to death. The women were passed around so much a dose was a foregone conclusion, or they were Cong sympathizers and inserted razor blades were they did irreparable damage to ones man hood. There is also the possibility of receiving a new strain of VD, venereal disease, this is not a boogey man type rumor this is fact, men are still listed as missing due to this exposure to an incurable strain that couldn't be allowed into the United States, these people were separated, and not allowed to return home to their families. Better to be reported missing then to share the shame of sexual activity away from the nest. More on this later.

The gunny and I ate well and drank more then our share, but maintained for my three day R&R, contrary to old woman tales that marines and sailors love to fight, when we can't find anyone to go fist city with we turn on each other. Sorry, not so. The gunny is a professional and had no time for such nonsense nor did I, I will say though that we did walk away from a few offers from newly arrived still wet behind the ears stateside commandos, they were in the right country to grow up in a hurry.

Word got out that I rounded up people missing without fanfare or muss and this is what I did before coming to Viet Nam. A Marine Major and a navy commander had me in for a meeting after my three days of R&R in Saigon, they had been in touch with my boss, the Admiral at CincPac in the Philippines and received permission to put my jaunt into Laos on hold and I was TAD, temporary additional duty, to their Saigon unit with berthing at the Navy barracks. This is where the first snag surfaced, because of my run in with the Chief in charge at said barracks that was not realistic, concessions were made and permission was given for me to remain at the marine barracks.

The job they asked of me was no different then what I'd been doing before Nam, but I did ask permission for three weeks notice before my run into Indian country up in Laos so to prepare myself to smell like a local when I sweat or perform other bodily functions, granted.

The next week was spent making myself known to the Navy and Army personnel at the local lockups, brigs and stockades. I was something new in the system and spent time explaining every time a fighting man is locked up beyond sobriety it interferes with the function of his unit and it's ability to perform in the field, having to go in country is punishment enough for any man. The word went out to all units as to my function and information was requested from one and all as to the whereabouts of their missing buddies, the word was, lets bring them in before they go too far and get their ass in a sling. The only penalty for missing from their unit or command was lockup long enough to determine their health both physically and mentally. The stress of combat and sometimes just the thought of being sent in harms way can stress some people out. Imagine being four months out of high school, you've had your basic military training and your dumped in a foreign country where every swinging dick is trying to get you killed or trying to kill you, you wonder now why some of these still wet behind the ears kids spook and skeedaddle. Put yourselves in their shoes then tell me our approach to discipline was too easy.

The Provost Marshall made available to me a small office in Headquarters Building and I mean small, put a swab and a broom in the space and I'd have to stand in the hall. Almost an hour into my new assignment and the bubble burst, in walks the local reps from the Naval Investigative Service with a stack of files for me, seems like they had it in their mind that I worked for them. The files had a wide variety of pending charges from theft, robbery, rape and general mayhem, looked to me as though they were giving me their failures and trying to get off the hook. Wrong move. I informed them of my stated agenda from the Admiral at CincPac and had no intention of playing detective, my primary function was finding and returning to duty the fellers who had gone on a walkabout.

They screamed and threatened even cajoled but to of no avail, the tug of war was about to begin. Two hours into my new assignment in walks the local Central Intelligence boys really ticked, they got nasty because I was supposed to be preparing for my trip into Laos, their threats sounded the same as the N.I.S. maybe they all read from the same spook book. They went to the commander then the Major who incidentally was a Mustang, one who came up through the ranks, and that was one tough bulldog bastard and built like a tank to boot, his name was Chisnel and he had ribbons from his shoulder to his kneecaps, a real no shitter, the prima donnas got no satisfaction and split, leaving me with the impression that they had just started to pull strings. Why me? Damn, when is this two years of easy duty I was promised going to start.

The major turned over to me eleven files of missing men, both Navy and Marines, time for me to go turn on the charm. No one ever said the job was going to be easy; they neglected to throw in heartbreak. My first case was a young marine who had wandered off the main thoroughfare, played with the wrong girl, had his throat cut, his genitals cut off and stuffed into his mouth and then was nailed to the side of a building spread-eagled for all river traffic to see.

Didn't say my job was pleasant. The information came to me by way of the Mama San from the small bar I decided to make my unofficial office and point of contact. I begged a small fund for information from the Marshals Office for the purpose of rewarding the locals for their help in locating missing personnel, this proved later to be the best move I could have made, even the local police and South Vietnamese regulars enjoyed the fruits of small rewards from time to time.

By giving the office results, I received the credit, but neglected to mention my fast growing large group of greedy informers, thus the reason for my finding the young marine the second day on the job. The kid had four days in Nam and was to leave with a squad to relieve a group that had their time in the bush, killed in the line of duty was the official word, lie, could anyone in good conscience write otherwise to the young marines family, I think not.

This case was cited and graphic for the express purpose not to shock, but to make the reader aware that being in a foreign country whether at war or not can be dangerous. Americans are not treated as the big brother that the news media portrays, we are disliked, even hated in some countries because of our attitude and a lot from our foreign policy, most feel as though we lord it over them and they resent being made to feel that way, consequently we have servicemen all over the world that are considered targets and fair game.

The following week after finding the young marine spread-eagled on the side of the barn was rather hectic with the marine barracks in an uproar yelling for blood and revenge on all slopes they could find, the Major had his hands full riding herd on one pissed off group, cooler heads prevailed, personnel was restricted to barracks until further notice and things leveled out, nothing like loss of liberty, shore leave, to get ones attention, three days seemed to be a sufficient cooling off period, time to return to business as usual.

After picking up a case of beer at the Barracks store, I made a beeline for my favorite watering hole to see what was shaking in the back streets of Saigon from my source of gossip, Mama San. Between giggles, she gave up two soldiers living in a hooch on the river about a mile upstream, she found it funny that they had set up housekeeping with no thought of female companions; the army didn't find it amusing. I spotted these two later the same afternoon after checking to see if in fact they were any of my business, bingo, they've been playing house for two weeks longer then their leave called for. I picked up two military police from the army, rented a small sampan for a run up to their little nest. The whole thing took less then twenty minutes from pick up to the stockade, the two were sent back stateside as undesirables and marked for discharge from the service. With the new policy on that behavior, if they had returned to duty nothing would have been said, they would have been cut some slack and life would have gone on.

Life wasn't all fun and frolic, once in awhile I was expected to check into the Navy liaison office at South East Asian headquarters, this is an experience one should not miss. I'd never met so many smart people in my life, the young Officers had an answer for everything and no experience to back it up, the fact that I was controlled by CincPac and an enlisted man to boot made me a target for clowns who wanted to exercise control over us lowlifes and prove their superior self. Knowing I would be on the move kept me from meeting these clowns some dark evening and kicking their superior teeth down their throat.

Major Chisnel USMC, caught up with me one day at the office and asked a small favor of me, seems one of his men refused to

return to barracks and was due to go in country and relieve the one thirty first sniper group. He was mean and drunk and had hurt three of his men already trying to get him to report in. His hangout was a dump on Full Moon Street called Long Life Bar, ya sure, that afternoon I paid the dump a visit. Sure enough my man was there larger then life, and I mean larger then life, drunk on his ass and in a mean mood, this is no time for diplomacy, all the nice guys I know are missing most of their teeth, this jewel had a baton he'd taken from the M.P's during one of his skirmishes, being a gentle soul, I came up on his blind side and hit him twice in the rib cage with my kubiton, a small stick looking affair, and once behind the ear. I heard the ribs give, a small fracture at best, not one to put him on the sick list, and down he went. I relieved him of his nightstick, cuffed him and went out the door looking for a patrol to transport him back to barracks. Fortunately one was handy and saved me an ass kicking, marines do not like to see other marines get their ass kicked, although not buddies with this clown there were about three ticked off individuals getting ready to take a bite out of my ass, they claimed I didn't fight fair, that may account for the fact why I still have my teeth.
Major Chisnel thanked me, then gave me hell for roughing up one of his marines, go figure.

My list of absentees was slowly diminishing, as was my popularity, I had one more person on my list. It was suggested that I consider a little R&R over in Bangkok, sounded good to me, not so to the spook community, they want anything, they want it now, what a sorry bunch of losers, why get off their ass and do it themselves when they've got a fish like me.

Pvt. Ayers, according to platoon records at Army Headquarters, was listed as a deserter and has been gone about three months that they know of, after checking with soldiers in his squad it seems he was KIA (killed in action). They remember bringing his remains from the firefight area to the evacuation zone and seeing his body tagged and put in a body bag, the only possibility I could come up with is some one changed places with Pvt. Ayers and ziggyed on out of Vietnam.

Records at Battalion had listed a Pvt. Lubbock KIA with the same dates, surprise, surprise, guess who was a company clerk, Lubbock it would seem had changed places with Ayers, wrote himself some new orders and split. The military runs on paperwork, tons of it, they probably generate enough paper in the course of a month to keep the furnaces of New York blazing to heat Manhattan for ninety days, so now the search begins. Its pretty simple really, Lubbock put his orders under the stack in his commanders in basket, when it comes up he reads the order number not the particulars, its just another rotation of personnel, thus we have Pvt. Lubbock going on rotation stateside and show Pvt. Ayers as a deserter. Can you imagine the pain and heartbreak of the Ayers family when the Army comes to their door searching for their son and marking him a deserter from a war zone, excuse me, I meant from a police action, horseshit, getting shot at is getting shot at, the hell with what name you give it.

Lubbock family is pretty much in the same boat, only their informed by the Army that their son is KIA, when he shows up on their doorstep someone's going to have a heart attack or if they had any sense they'd kick the hell out of the bastard, throw him out of the house, and call the authorities.

Now that I was a thorn in everyone's side and had endeared myself to the Commanding clan, all they wanted to see was the back of my head as I got on a plane out of their area, spooks Ville still wanted me and was doing the slow burn because I was granted two weeks in Bangkok starting immediately. I knew the chance of my being bumped off the flight were slim to none, gees, it's hell being popular.

After saying my good-byes in town and thanking the Marines for the use of their barracks, I was driven to the airstrip where I was booked on a direct flight to Bangkok. My driver was Major Chisnel, his way of thanking me was to jam a bottle of Crown Royal into my kit and wish me luck.

This was a direct flight to Bangkok's Don Muang airport, we were greeted by a friendly customs officer who directed me to the transportation desk, and I could have taken an air conditioned limo instead of the crowded bus, what the hell, when in Rome.

My destination was Pattaya (Pattyeye) eighty-five miles southeast of Bangkok. This is the largest beach resort in the Asian tropics, known to all visiting servicemen as the spot with sandy beaches, lots of bars, and the loveliest women in all of Asia, the Thais love this spot and have seen to it that it does not become a Mecca for prostitutes. Until you've ridden a bus for two and a half hours in the heat of Asia loaded down with Thais you haven't lived, the people are polite and bend over backwards to see to your comfort and treat everyone as though they've known you all your life, they hold the Americans in high esteem and it shows.

Trouble seems to follow me as though it was metal and I was the magnet. The driver of our bus was unloading the luggage when the familiar old cry of stop thief sounds, different language same sound of distress. Sure enough here comes the culprit sprinting right for me with a bag and bright color directly behind him who turned out to be the owner, a female no bigger then a minute but showing no quit. Being handy I backhanded the thief and was impressed with his ability to somersault and land on his head. The young lady in question grabbed her bag and walked away in a huff, I was not so lucky, seems the local police frown on physical assault on its citizens, thief or not, that's their job.

They took me to the police station, read me the riot act, thanked me, then drove me to a beach hotel where they checked me in as a friend and visiting officer, the rate was fantastic as was the room. I had a view from my balcony of the ocean and direct access to the beach, now this is living. Never being happy, I sulked a bit due to the fact I was an hour behind schedule of having a drink and a dip in the ocean, the usual O'Brian luck was holding, the ocean was full of jellyfish, guess I should have checked the migration of the damn things before I came here, I settled for the drink at the outdoor bar and some sun.

After the first week of sun and rest, the inactivity was getting to me, there were other servicemen at the resort and on the beach but you can only tell so many sea stories before you find yourself repeating yourself.

Every day found me at the local fish pier, I had hired the boat for half days for the week for fishing, my luck was good and each day I gave the crew my catch, this gave them extra money, they sold the fish to the local hotel and took a couple home for themselves.

The crew knew I was due to leave, they threw me a small party at the Skippers home and it was amazing to see how many kids those three guys had. When I told the hotel I was leaving for Bangkok for my last week in Thailand they volunteered to make reservations for me at a nice hotel in Bangkok, I left it in their capable hands after explaining my limited finances.

Loading on the bus for my return trip I was surprised to see my new friends the fishermen and families and two of the local police, I didn't know whether the police were saying goodbye or making sure I got out of Dodge, it was a good feeling anyway.

On arrival at the bus depot in Bangkok, I was greeted by a big placard with my name, the Hotel had sent a driver for me, at this point I knew I was in deep kimchee, this Hotel must cost a fortune. I was driven to the Oriental on 48 Oriental Lane right on the Chao Phya river, maybe one night at these prices then I'll look around for something cheaper, check-in was a surprise, the rate was the same as my Pattaya room, so look a gift horse in the mouth why don't you.

Before leaving the front desk low and behold the local police were there to say hello, they were very polite and should I need anything, they were at my disposal. I was beginning to think that I'd stopped Dillenger in commission of a crime. The room looked out on the river and had a great balcony overlooking the pool, the small mini bar was a big hit with me as well, it didn't take me long to have a cold one, a week of this I can handle.

The information desk was most helpful in locating a local that had a cab service both on the water and land, I was going to become a sightseer my last week. The fellow came over to the hotel, after we went over the tour books we eliminated all the temples, except the great Buddha, the government buildings and museums, the waterways was one of my interest, Thai kick boxing and some nice pubs, no problem. One driver was assigned to me after we fixed a price for the week, rather then have the guy stay in the car or on the boat while I did my thing, I had him join me for company, he knew his way around and we got on well.

After three days we were driving by the thieves market off the river Chao Phya when I spot some military personnel going into a bar called The Yankee, nothing will do but I have to check the place out, I'll cut to the chase, what a dump.

We received dirty looks when we walked in, my driver said he'd wait outside, nonsense, we'll have a Thai beer called Tiger Piss, the American bartender said, we don't serve Thais, amazing say's I considering your a guest in their country, all of a sudden the whole place is standing and all I can think is Jesus, I've got a big mouth.

The murmuring started but as luck would have it I was recognized by one of the marines from Major Chisnels platoon from Vietnam on R&R, he whispered to his buddies he wanted no part of this shit, he told them he saw what happened to the last marine I returned to duty. I also heard the word, Phantom, first time I heard I had a nickname, the word got around and the temperature slowly dropped, my Thai friend almost quit sweating and we were left to our beer.

The bartender was a skuzball of the first order, one of the wannabees of the soldier of fortune ilk who just never measured up. His attitude remained the same as when we entered, shitty. Our next beer was slammed down hard enough to slop some over on my person, politely I asked for a bar towel to clean up, the laugh was enough to piss me off. I didn't like the prick anyway, he told me to go to a bathhouse if I was such a pussy, leaning over the bar was his second mistake. Shit, I hate would be bullies and tough guys, he wasn't that heavy as I drug him over the bar and slapped him in the teeth a few times, at this point my driver/tour guide was ready to get with the program and was covering my back. It all happened so fast no one made a move or said a word. Numb nuts was out of the picture for awhile but two of his equally looking scruffy bastard buddies wanted to take up the challenge, not wanting to spend the remainder of my R&R in the slammer I tried to back down and call it quits, not to be. This attitude on my part told them it was fear and they wanted to push it, the one with the knife was my only concern, the other plug ugly was just another punk of a follower.

While touring the city I'd invested in a couple of throwing knives, illegal as hell as a guest in a foreign country, but, what the hell, before the heroes could fan out on me I reached behind my neck where I kept a chamois carrier on a thong for one of the knives, the other I carried in a specially sewn pocket inside my pants at the waist, the first throw was in the center of their table just to get their attention, which it did, I pulled the second out of my waist and just held it, the trouble was over right now.

Time to get while the getting was good, my driver said nothing, however he did look rung out. It was still early in the afternoon but I told him to split for the day and I'd see him tomorrow, no argument there.

After checking the desk for messages I went to the room and put on swim trunks and headed for the pool for some fun in the sun. Shadows across my closed eyes had me look up to two big Americans who didn't look too friendly, they were pleasant enough, introduced themselves working for the US Government, that told me who they were. I was invited to the American Embassy right now, declined, can't do that, bet me, maybe tomorrow, that is not how that works, they were at a loss as to how to handle this situation, intimidation, didn't work, finally they gave up and said they'd call later. Their fearless leader called instead and read me the riot act, or at least started too, I hung up on him, called the front desk and refused any more calls for the rest of the day.

At the hotel's riverside terrace I was enjoying their barbecue dinner, which I understood they were famous for, and I had company, I wasn't about to get indigestion from the uninvited guest so I said, either join me and be quiet, or leave a note at the front desk with your phone number and reason for bugging me and maybe I'll get back to you, smoke coming out of an individuals ears was new to me but not interesting enough to spoil my dinner. The message must have hit home, I was invited for a drink in the lounge after my dinner, and he'd wait.

He was from the Embassy and his title was trade commissioner, and I'm the king of the hobos, these guys seem to come from the same mold, talk alike, look alike and seem to think alike, but they all smell the same, CIA.

I was told the people back in Saigon were nervous and wanted me back in the area post haste, he was informed I don't work for you people so get off my ass, then the threats started all over again. I told the self important ass to call my boss at CincPac and clear it with him, after all I'm only an enlisted man who takes orders, he was at least smart enough to see when he was in a no win situation and settled down and enjoyed his drink and the atmosphere.

The thing that bothered him was me staying in such a high rent hotel, then he said something that really pissed me off, "All the money the guys over in Saigon gave you to keep the local informants happy didn't all go to that purpose right,"

"Before I bounce you on your ass shithead let me set the record straight, those two clowns in Saigon layed a couple of hundred bucks in American on and that's all, if they claimed more then I suggest you check their bank balances, accuse me again and we'll go see the man and let him make the determination where the loot is going." As red faced as he was he didn't get a chance to reply, two local members of the police department in civvies were at the table asking me if everything was all right, where they came from I have no idea or why, but they were welcome, they told me they were in the lobby should they be needed, with that they left. Mr. CIA was sitting with his mouth hanging open and looking at me with that just stepped in dogshit look.

Seems to me I was just afforded a new status of respect; he asked how did I know the local constabulary. I had to say I honestly didn't know, it was a good feeling though. I'll bet the wires would be hot tonight between Bangkok and Washington, good, it's about time I received some recognition and was made maybe an Admiral, lucky if I don't end up in Portsmouth prison more like it.

Mr. CIA left after another drink, which I stuck him for, he said he'd see me in the morning. I said I don't think so, leave a note at the front desk with a number and we'll see about getting together. I knew I was pushing my luck, but screw him and his company, shit I hate being pushed around, titles don't mean a damn to me and never have, it ticks me off to have people look down their noses at me just because they have a title and work for the government. The only reason they do that is because they're too lazy to work and to dumb to steal, maybe this attitude accounts for me always being in deep shit.

Enough excitement for one day, I sat on the balcony of my room after assaulting the rooms mini bar and enjoyed a nice quiet brandy with one hell of a view, it doesn't get any better then this.

At breakfast I was joined by the two plain cloths policemen from the night before, I asked them if they ever slept or did they just stay up all night, I got the impression that my humor was lost on them. These people have a different slant on life then the

Americans, their very dedicated people with a fierce pride in their accomplishments and their country.

Before I put my foot in my mouth, again, I invited them to join me for breakfast, from the look on their faces that was something unheard of, after a bit of coaxing they joined me, had no idea what to order so I asked if I could do the honors, making sure bacon or ham was not against their religion. We had a nice visit and refrained from talking business until our second cup of coffee. They were sent by their chief who had heard of my little foray into the Yankee club and wanted to see me, shit, here we go, they assured me I was not facing arrest, nor was I in anyway in trouble or disfavor, and they would consider it a favor if I would join them. They had no idea how long I would be after I expressed my concern for my waiting driver however, they did say that they would make a car and driver available to me after the meeting for the remainder of the day, such a deal. I told the driver to take the day off with pay and see me in the morning and join me for breakfast, he and I were becoming fast friends and he voiced his concern about police business, he was told no problem and to relax.

The chief was short of stature, wiry and very well groomed with a pleasant manner to boot, he thanked me for coming and didn't know what to make of the fact that I treated his men to breakfast, very un-American, does this attitude give you any idea what they think of the ugly American, take heed, the world is shrinking and we are fast becoming isolationist, wake up America!

The chief started the ball rolling by asking about the incident at the Yankee club, and again showed surprise when I mentioned them not wanting to serve a local, he did get a bit red, these clowns are now marked for deportation, bet ya, anyone want to buy a club cheap. He wanted to see the knives I illegally carried and heard I was so handy with, I asked if I was in trouble, he replied, he felt we were on the same side of the law, encouraging, this opened the ball, down to business, Americans were a great source of income and much needed hard currency, on the whole, were pretty well behaved, come spend their money and return to wherever. Then we have the ex-servicemen who return to our country and are somewhat a blight on our society, some have bars which are legitimate and thriving, other bars sell drugs and harbor the so called mercenary soldier of fortune who is nothing more then a ner'-do-well who is a leech and a thief, womanizer and a drunk. The purpose of this visit is to ask you if you could remain for a short while to help my force to identify the bad eggs and the source of the drugs so that we can sort out the good from the bad.

The only answer I could give was to say I would be more then happy to hang around if permission would be given from my boss in the Philippines, there is another agency that seems to think they have dibs on my services within a week or so, the Chief was not to be put down so quickly, I don't know who he called, but after I gave him the Admirals number he wasted no time, he suggested lunch and we took off for my hotel, guess he thought I only ate at fancy joints. My stock at the hotel soared as I walked in with the man; he carried a lot more weight then I had originally thought. The phone call came in the middle of lunch for the Chief, he was all smiles and shook my hand and welcomed me aboard, the power of intercountry politics is amazing. I was due to leave Sunday, this was Friday, I was told I would be picked up Monday morning for a briefing at his office, he would inform my driver and his boss that their services would still be needed, all bills to be sent to the Chiefs office, next stop the front desk, same routine, no limit on service, all bills to be sent to the Chief starting immediately, my kind of guy. While saying goodbye and explaining I was not a miracle worker, the Desk Manager called my name and pointed me out to a couple of very impressive looking gentlemen, who turned out to be none other then the American Ambassador and his assistant, he welcomed me to Bangkok and said his office was available should I need anything during my stay, I introduced him to the Chief, to his credit he was very cordial.

The note left in my room box was from the Ambassador, clearly stating should anything go amiss during my activities, the Embassy would deny any knowledge or involvement as to my presence in Bangkok, nice safe attitude for a career diplomat.

Monday morning had me on the move locating hangouts for the bad boys of the thieves market, and to see how the hell I was going to separate the good from the bad, then what, I'm playing this all by ear. As usually is the case, ex-or former military men love to talk about their days on active duty, some of the stories have them performing amazing feats and superhuman daring-dos.

Let's see if I can roust these assholes into an ego trip, let's start with "When I was in the zone" what the fuck are you talking about, automatically your a fucking phony, our life in country was something indescribably painful, not a trip you'd talk about easily.

I've come to believe that I'm here because I'm a throwaway, when you work for the Navy you better get your shit together, we're not known for humility. The Admiral wants me to kickass, and that is what I'm going to do, I love the area I'm in, but, I have no conscience when it comes to comfort, especially my own.

The word was out, I was in Bangkok to kick ass for the military, search out the deserters and AWOL's who decided they disliked Viet Nam enough to remain alive in Bangkok and make their way the best they knew how, booze, broads and drugs. This didn't endear them to the locals, which was to work to my benefit; I had no trouble locating people or their hangouts because of the informers who wanted the Americans out of their business. I was able to locate weapon stashes, drugs and hidy-holes for illegals. My success did not go unnoticed, the local police were having a high old time and deporting people as fast as they could count, the military was picking people up as they disembarked from the planes with ongoing tickets, not everyone was happy with me though, the bullet holes on my balcony and in my room attested to that, time for me to confront these assholes, before someone gets lucky.

Bangkok has a criminal element of its own, the Police would go to any lengths to eliminate this unwelcome faction in their Town and Country, and at the moment I was their fair-haired boy, should I want something, all I had to do was ask. Simtex is a contribution to the world from the Yugoslavs and more powerful then TNT, my request for a few ropes with some pencil timers was no problem, in fact, they delivered enough to wipe out the whole of Downtown Bangkok, most of this I stashed at the police armory, I had plans for a couple of ropes, along with the pencil timers I also asked for and received some radio controlled detonators, payback time.

Being no stranger to black bag operations, I let myself into the Yankee Club in the wee hours of the morning and went to work. First a small circle of rope (Simtex) under the favorite table of the tough guys with a detonator, next a line under the bar with another detonator, this should get their attention.

Later, in the middle of the day, I reentered the club and could feel the freeze, just because I'd shit on their business was no reason to be outright hostile, surely they can't be missing the scumbags that I had been responsible for leaving the country, there's just no accounting for some peoples taste.

As luck would have it the boys were having what looked like a council of war, all the better, I gave them my best speech about leaving the country while they still could, the response was a few visible knives and some weapons, my good buddy the bartender had a mean looking AKA next to his leg, talking time was evidently over. With a press of the button on my detonator facing the table it disintegrated, last I saw of the table it was heading for the sky, reaction time from the bar was a bit slow, it went the way of the table, the bartender went the other way, not thinking too clearly, I was a bit slow in clearing the area, talk about hanging around to admire your work, it cost me my eyebrows and I had what looked like a damn nice sunburn. Now to convince the Embassy I was elsewhere, with the help of the police they had me in Pattaya at the time of the explosion, explained the sunburn.

The Yankee club was demolished, the denizen were ready to leave the country as soon as they were released from the hospital, others in and around Bangkok involved in illegal enterprise were looking to the horizon for greener pastures, the Chief of Police swore his undying gratitude and threw me one hell of a dinner at the hotel. All was not roses however, the note from the Embassy was telling me I was persona non grata, now is that gratitude or what. The note further stated that I was to enjoy myself for twenty-four hours, I would be picked up at the hotel and escorted, not transported, to the airport where a military aircraft would deposit me back in Viet Nam, shit, there's no justice.
Later I was to receive word that my visit was fruitful inasmuch as I got the ball rolling in getting most of the scumbag mercenaries to relocate, all was not in vain.

Being the gracious bastard that I'm normally, I took a great deal of delight of shitting in everyone's mess kit, stuff you, I'm headed for the pit of no recognition, officers of outstanding rank who make no mistakes, this is spelled with a capitol "fuck you", the fools in charge give you pause to wonder, do this, do that, after you've dealt a stunning blow to our side, then it's time to get even, do it to the other side. People from the Academies have been doing studies on confrontations since time in the colonies, again, I'd like to point out that they are all assholes, get it on, and win, there is no room for wishy-washy individuals or closet queens, kick ass now or get out of my way.

Time spent in Bangkok was something one would never forget, the friends I'd met and the feeling of closeness is something the average person would have problems accepting as fact.

The return to the base on the river with the small craft was a real clusterfuck, landing at Saigon, I was met by a contingent of marines bent on the purpose of arrest for AWOL, kiss my ass, talk about the military lack of communication, so much for meeting operational standards.

After forty-eight hours of bullshit, thank god for the Major in charge of operations, he put a call in to the Admiral in Subic, wow, did the shit hit the fan, it's easy to say, Ha Ha, got ya. Keep in mind the mindless fucks in charge, called officers, surround you and take turns keeping the mind set wound up to the point you are out in the cold and always at their mercy, so much for friends in high places.

Before I could say," let's have a cold beer," the boy's representing Christians in Action were on my doorstep, let your imagination run when you picture my sandbagged hooch with a doorstep, fall down inside the damn thing and you'd break your fool neck. The boys were all business and got to the problem at hand without any prelims, seems that infiltration from across the border had increased at an alarming rate and more up to date information was needed. You guessed it, yours truly was volunteered by the Admiral when he found that charges were pending against me in Bangkok. This of course was the work of the not so undercover group working out of the American Embassy in Bangkok with the aid of the ball-less military attaché who worried more about his evals and promotions, real gutless asshole, you guessed it, a lifer from the academy. Without fanfare they laid their request out for me to head on into the elephant grass heading for the border of Cambodia and do what I do best, snoop. Their instructions were to leave yesterday, well friend, it doesn't work that way, that's my ass hanging out for all to kick and I'm not going to make it easy for anyone, after all the booze and rich food still in me from Bangkok, any unfriendliness could smell me coming from a mile away, I needed at least six weeks to clear my system eating local food and drink, not bad, they gave me one. I'm not too sure that this wasn't an attempt to rid the area of the Admirals fair-haired boy.

After a week of isolation, no showers, shaving or practicing personal hygiene as known to civilized peoples, I was given my marching orders, knives sharpened and rice balls in my sack, I was off, not quite. I was given a radio to carry that would give the average man a hernia and told to report in twice a day, yah sure, my regular means of communications had disappeared, a small imager, satellite controlled and instant readouts, impossible to locate the operator, the pric 25 radio was left in the toolies as soon as I cleared the area, if I carried that son of a bitch, in less time then it takes to send one message I'd be dead. Fuck the jerks, I give them a full report if and when I make it back, this came from the numb nuts clear out of the area back in air conditioned offices who specialize in cluster fucks. Most times following orders can shorten you life, I'm a loner with only myself to worry about, otherwise team work and covering each others backs is your only chance for survival.

My usual isolation time had been drastically reduced for this operation, my ass was sucking wind and the hair on the back of my neck was stiffer then the hair on a boars back.

This was a trip with no support and less transportation, it took me three days before I crossed into Cambodia and still a nervous wreck, I spent more time covering my back trail then advancing. I slithered through the mud every chance I got hoping to eliminate any telltale smells of easy living, damned if I couldn't smell myself, if I could you can bet your teenage ass the unfriendlies could too. Luck was with me so far, no way could that last, that feeling of dread was stronger then ever.

Five days into the foray, activity was on the increase in the distance, I'd circled the area and came in from the backside of the trail I was to report on, my habit was to sleep high up, preferably a tree with extending branches for fast egress as an ass saving method of departure, wrong this time, morning brought a large massing of little brown men in pith helmets and big guns, weapons to you professionals, O.K. smart ass.
What now? This wasn't your ordinary bunch of farmers or Khmer Rouge, these were regulars trained by the Chinese up North from the way they conducted themselves and went about setting up perimeters. They were traveling light, well armed and meant business, this is what I was sent out to find out, so now I could either sit there and continue to wet my pajamas, or face reality, make my move and die like the dummy I felt like for being caught in my present position. The will to survive won out, the usual weak spot of defense failed to point itself out to me, like over here, fortunately the tree coverage was thick and heavy and presented no problems to scurrying about, someone up there likes me, my guardian angel was working overtime.

The sky's opened and a real gully washer poured down, before I got out of there I was sure I was going to be presumed drowned and missing in action.

At first the Viet Cong Regulars just hunkered down to wait out the weather tucked into their ponchos, bad move, we were in hilly terrain and the water was really moving, it wasn't long before the troops were wading knee deep in a real quagmire, they started looking for high ground and moving out enmasse, Amen to that, I had visions of them crawling all over the treetops, didn't happen.

The only thought going through my mind was to pull a quick disappearing act and have tea with these boys at some other time. It seemed like forever before I felt safe enough and had put some distance between me and the unfriendly campers before I felt safe enough to drop down out of the trees, I headed for the hills close to the water to dig myself a hidey hole, visibility was zilch and there were a few areas to be checked out, just now, the job is only partly done.

Early the next day I awoke to a rumbling, hell, I thought it was my stomach, wrong, before I could say shit; I was speeding down the hillside in a mudslide. The ground overnight had become saturated and definitely unstable, this was enough to make a Christian out of Attila the Hun. This was it, I was sure, so I went with the flow, little play on words, luck had me stopped on the rivers edge with barely enough of my face out of the muck to enable me to survive. Movement was not an option open to me, I was rolled up nice and tight to the point my arms and legs were firmly set and held immobile. Later this was to be the cause of many a sleepless night, cold sweats and breathlessness, although only a couple of hours in this position, it seemed an eternity. Before the rains came again I can't say my whole life passed before my eyes, but the anger I felt at being immobilized, and the fear due to the inability to help myself, was so great, if I could have pulled the pin, I probably would have. The tears on my face surprised me, not being an emotional person, I was stunned,Ha, I was relieved to find that it was the rain. This is what awoke me from an exhausted sleep. First my left arm was washed clear of mud and allowed me enough freedom of movement to uncover the rest of me, then and there I damned near scrubbed the mission.

The rains one more day then the sky cleared up, my body was one mass of bruises; sure beat the alternative, I moved out on the double.

Scoping out the Ho Che Minh Trail was a bit scary. Damn, there was a lot of movement in the area and I'd seen just about everything I was asked to report on, getting ready to depart the area, I noticed in the area in the distance, a stockade type structure, in for a penny in for a pound, the area was heavily grown over with trees and brush, so, why not.

What I was expecting I had no idea. From my position I could see that the compound held prisoners, whether American or not, I wasn't close enough to make that determination, security was really tight, my best move was to scoot on out of there and hit the trail. I'd already been in the area longer then prudent trying to get a head count.

For three days I shadowed the trail and found three other camps similar to the first up the trail, don't try to guess what the camps were there for, I'll tell you. Americans being considered softies, gave the Viet Cong the idea that if they built their stockade's on the Ho Che Minh trail and filled them with American prisoners and their allies, we wouldn't have the balls to bomb or strafe their supply dumps.

They were proven wrong, the trail was the target for runs by bombers who dropped their cluster bombs all up and down this supply route, a bomb knows no race, friend, or foe, it is built for one thing, and when dropped, does it's job, gives one pause for thought as to the MIA question.

Still upset over what I'd seen, and as one man, could do nothing about, I became a bit slack as to my own safety and vigilance, something that should have been foremost in my mind at all times. My wakeup call came when I took one in my left leg, fleshy part and high, to give you an Idea, if that slope had aimed a bit further to his right, I'd be singing soprano. Amazing how fast you can run when the choice is stand still and take another or, move out and save your ass, running like the wind I felt as though I was flying, damned if I wasn't, these boys had set an ambush and a few booby traps, hell, I must have been seen after all.

The explosion threw me through the air, that I hit a tree trunk hard enough to scramble my noodle, but not enough to put me down, I was up and running through that brush faster then castor oil through a sick monkey, man, that's moving. I cleared the area and it was awhile before I slowed down to assess the damage, luck was with me, the wound in the upper thigh went clean through, looked like a piece of shrapnel buzzed across my knee cap and gave me a nasty gash, didn't seem life threatening at the time. Traveling light, I don't carry a medical kit, couple of Band-Aids, sulfur powder and a bandanna, took a little time to administer field first aid, with any luck I lost these clowns and could maybe make the border by dark, find the river and hitch a ride on into base, at this point the wounds were showing signs of red in the area of entry.

Hell, anyone that knows me knows that I get lost a block from home; my sense of direction is non-existent. I'd anticipated about three days to the river, horseshit, I was further then I thought, like about two days, my fever was running high, both wounds had become infected, nice, one in each leg, not surprising considering that the Viet Cong dipped the tips of their bullets in human feces for just that purpose. Dizziness was no problem, hell, it just felt like an evening out in Saigon after a little R&R.

Don't know how long I'd been out, but when I came to, I had a banana leaf across my kisser, when I removed it I was looking at the ugliest stranger I'd ever seen, the meanest craziest son-of-a-bitch I'd ever had the good fortune to run across. He found me on the trail, drug me into his underground hidey-hole where we spent four days hiding and waiting for my fever to break, (might explain my claustrophobia. When we did hit the trail, he never tired of telling me what a sorry ass I was and how damn stupid I was for being seen by those sorry nearsighted slopes we were fighting.

My savior was all that was left of a platoon of regular Army scouts on a fact-finding mission; his expertise was that of a sniper. On our run out of Indian country, he time and again showed his ability, he thought I was a bit weird since all I carried was throwing knives, later at close quarters when I was able to prove the virtue of the throwing knife, he relented somewhat and got off my ass, a little bit anyway.

My three-day guesstimate turned into a week, in the meantime, my traveling companion told me his story. As the lone survivor of his recon platoon he went dinky dou. He had no thought of living beyond killing his next slope, he'd been in Indian country long enough to be considered KIA, POW, or MIA. Other then a grandmother who raised him, he had no other family back in the states, his goal at present was to be killed in action and joining his buddies, we had quite a discussion in that area. I made it quite clear that I had no intention of joining the man down in hell and carrying a pitchfork throughout eternity, he let me know that he thought I was a wimp.

He was raised in Baltimore by his grandmother, after he had worn out his welcome in a bunch of foster homes. His juvenile record was a humdinger but not bad enough to keep him out of the Army after Viet Nam started, those were the days you had to be in your grave to be considered 4-F and unfit to serve your country, this was one hell of a soldier.

His biggest concern was being sent back stateside on our return to base, maybe even being considered a deserter in time of war. Seeing as how he saved my bacon, we concocted a story that he and I had been together ever since my entry into Indian country and I recruited him to assist me in my mission, let's hope my Marine Major friend can see his way clear to buy into this story. Dex's main desire was to stay in Asia, preferably, Bangkok, maybe, just maybe we can accommodate him, I had a few markers I could call in from that area.

Damn near seven days on the run for the border we were spotted by an air rescue chopper making a sweep for survivors of a recent crash of a Navy recon plane. We were grateful for the lift and we were deposited on the deck of the USS Ranger, Air Craft Carrier, we came as a surprise as no one was listed to be even close to being in that area, we were finally cleared and given clean cloths and quarters.

Man, do those Airedales have it made, clean sheets, gedunk and pogy bait till hell wont have it, two days of that and we had the worst case of the runs you could ever imagine. All that fresh water and rich food did us in, out in the toolies that's all a guy thinks of, the normal one's anyway, ice cream, cake, pies, big roast with lots of gravy smothered in vegetables, makes for happy thoughts, in reality we had to revert to a diet of steamed rice, fish and veggies, talk about heartbreak.

After three days of cruising, word came to transport Dex and I to home base by helo, the party was over. Man oh man did they ever come after us in droves, Navy brass, Army big shots, last but not least, the Christians in Action(CIA).

We went through more checkups at the Navy sickbay at my base of operations at Quang Tri, damn did that place look shabby after the spit and polish of the carrier.

Lt. Horse's ass was still holding down his desk at headquarters. Awaiting his next evaluation, he's one of those officers that make me wish I'd been thrown out of the Navy. Major Chisnel of the Marines Corps was on hand to help me through the bullshit from the CIA and NIS, he saw that we had some breathing room before making our report and sneaking in my Army buddy Dex.

At this time my report was gone over with a fine toothcomb, and for the most part treated as myth or just plain bullshit. According to the experts in Asian affairs I made the whole thing up, I had never left the country and I hadn't seen shit. I wrote my report in a whorehouse in Saigon just to justify my absence, this is the way any report is treated by the brass when their asshole troops come in from the field and report no activity in the area. Any other report to the contrary is nonsense, of course they were pissed at me to start, I'd failed to report in as scheduled, they hadn't heard from me for so long they figured I'd bought it. I found out later that no order had gone out to search for one lone Irishman that had been missing for awhile, don't get me started on the clean pressed fatigue wearing rear echelon mothers without a clue as to what the hell was going on where the action was.

All I received for my trouble was a royal ass chewing for failure to report while in the field, go figure, my wounds were ignored, again they figured I received them in some alley in Saigon.

The infection was gone from my scratches and I was in no danger of losing my limbs, I was given a clean bill of health from the Navy doctors and authorized two weeks of R&R. My now constant companion and buddy Dex was given the same papers, we decided on Bangkok, that's one place the locals like me and the American Embassy declared me persona non grata. Major Chisnel promised to play games with my papers for a week or so, on word from me he was to deep six Dex's papers and he would no longer exist as far as Uncle Sam was concerned.

Like a couple of thieves in the night we entered Bangkok as quietly as we knew how, we started to party. It wasn't long before the booze took hold of Dex, he'd been dry for better then four months now and one beer was the equal of a mule kick. Hell, we hadn't even checked into our hotel yet and we'd already left a trail of busted heads and irate bar owners and bar girls with black and blue pinched rumps to mark our progress to our digs.

We were swooped down upon by six very serious looking, ass kicking capable, officers of the law. I know I'm good, Dex thinks he's better and changes clothes in a phone booth, in this case a cool head better prevail, Dex was calmed down and accepted our escort, surprise, we were sent to the very hotel I'd checked out of months before, very spendy and definitely out of our price range.

After being deposited in a large room with a view, our only orders were to call room service for what we desired, but to remain in our room until the following day. Later we were to learn the wisdom of that order, the crowd we left in our wake was just short of being a lynch mob.

My old friend, Soo Wang heard over his cab radio about a couple of runaway servicemen having too much fun drinking and kicking ass, later he told me, "Only one person I know who shows so much disrespect for the law. Pappy must be back from Viet Nam," He was later to tell me that the word went out, if in fact it was his old friend, the crazy American, and any harm came to him, the people involved were in deep kimchee. The local police got the word to lighten up, at this point everyone was guessing, but pretty sure only one person fit the description of the overzealous American.

Next morning Dex knew we were heading for the brig and a rather nasty time from the local endarmes, surprise, breakfast in bed, a bucket of beer from room service gave him pause.

The Police came into the suite and asked if we needed anything, no, O.K. they had work to do, in walks the man mountain dean, my former driver, and body guard, courtesy of the local triad boss who felt he owed me a favor. What's a couple of bombed out bars between friends? Told me I was invited to dinner the following evening at his home, I apologized for the imposition but asked for an invitation for my buddy Dex as well. This was to be the start of a money-making relationship for Dex and the local triads.

The only ducking I did while in Bangkok was from the CIA, they were having kittens trying to find out what the hell I was up to in Bangkok, to this day I've never told them, never will, fuck em.

Next morning, bright and early Dex and I were awoken by the hotel masseuse, followed by room service, our schedule was laid out for us and we were literally swept out of the hotel, man, this was really impressive to Dex. Little did he know that the people responsible for the cloak and dagger moves were to be his future employers.

In the meantime, my boss the Admiral was shittin' kittens, everyone wanted a piece of my ass and the flack was really flying. I'd disappeared from the hospital, left the country, and was due to give a report to the Admiral and his ass kissing staff back in the Philippines, word came to me from the Bangkok police who were dummying up as to my whereabouts, time to do what I came here to do and clear the area.

Playing the man who wasn't there was really becoming hard work; the Bangkok police knew their business. Dex and I were snuck out of the country under the cover of darkness and flown up to Singapore, where we were met by the Islands finest, they were undercover police seldom seen and less talked about. They were well aware of Dex and his wanting to remain in Asia in some form of police work, and as a productive member of their society to earn his keep.

Promises were made, all Dex had to do, was to show what he could do to help rid the straits of the pirate threat to shipping. The pirates of the straits of Malaga were fast becoming a force unto themselves, bolder and bolder inhibiting the normal flow of traffic, this job was offered to me months before. My responsibilities as a Navy man eliminated me from the running, not so with my buddy Dex. With a bit of help from the local Navy, we took out a couple of fast moving gun boats with fifties, thirties, two 81's fore and aft, grenade launchers, M-16's and for good measure, two hard driving 79's (in the shoulder that is.) Our first excursion into pirate country was quiet, two nights later the shit hit the fan, Dex had a feel for this kind of attack, and attack he did.

He caught three boats with their sterns unprotected and came upon them with nary a sound, no muss, no fuss. His crew commandeered the vessels, turned their crews over to the Singapore police quietly to eliminate any future warnings. It would be a few weeks before the pirates of the Straits noticed the thinning out of their comrades. Dex was so effective right from the get go that the local good guys adopted him as one of their own, I can quit worrying about him now, I'd best get my ass back to the Philippines.

There were no farewell parties from Bangkok this time, my buddy Soo Wang met me when I got off the boats and took me to the air terminal by the back way, the Chief of Police was waiting to say goodbye and in passing said that the U.S. Embassy was curious as to my whereabouts, no one knew, what a mystery, I had orders to destroy the Thailand Diplomatic passport upon arrival in the Philippines.

Upon arrival I was met by the Thai rep in Manila, shuttled down to Northern Luzon to the town of Olongopo, just outside of the US Naval base. I dropped in to see my old friend Susan Yee at 24 Magsaysay, renewed old acquaintances and then snuck on the base before reveille the next morning.

Now I guess I can tell the Admiral how I managed to come and go and disappear so readily. The river skirting the Naval Base and the town of Olongopo is known as shit river, this is the town's sewage, up river at the end of the base where the dump is, base dump referred to by the locals as the gold mine, closely monitored and controlled by the local bent nose society of thugs, traffic is by permission only and for a sum, you have no idea what goodies the Navy and Marines throw away.

The big fence at that end of the base has a hole in it so big, you could drive a tank through it. Being well known around town as a fair man and a friend of the local police, catching a ride across the river was not a problem, I've never had a problem with ferry service.

When I appeared out of nowhere, the Admiral had mixed emotions (to say the least) surprise, wonder, the most outstanding emotion seemed to be hate, can't blame him, all along I've broken all the rules that he has held dearly for the past twenty five years of service to his beloved U.S.Navy.

The heat coming down from Washington, Bupers, (Bureau of personnel) and the Naval hospital concerning my follow up treatment and welfare was more then he wanted to put up with right now, the CIA wanted a few words with me as well.

Now being a lousy time to kill me, the Admiral relented, called off his Marine squad of hit men and granted me sick leave of forty five days, good for me, bad for the State of Idaho and the Town of Ketchum.

The deal was for me to finish my period of sick leave, return to Treasure Island Naval Base in San Francisco, CA. and receive my medical discharge, and sure, I have a bridge for sale in Arizona, lying bastards one and all.

Book Two-- The Sellout!!

Here I am living every sailors dream, except for those that think they want to be chicken farmers, living in a resort town, lots of female companionship, working as a bartender, easy money and great tips, who walks in to spoil the dream of a lifetime, the Airedale Ordinance Chief who convinced me the Navy couldn't get along without in the first place, then gets my sorry ass shipped to Viet Nam. My first thought is to kick the bastards ass and throw him out of the bar, common sense prevails, I'm still in the Navy, the large manila envelop under his arm has my attention, why do I feel as though I've just had a finger wave without benefit of a salve.

"Chief, don't tell me that those are orders for me under your arm, there really my medical discharge papers, right."

"Wrong mister, these are your new orders from CincPac," (Commander-In -Chief, Pacific, Philippines.)

This is one of those times when you should rap a towel around your neck to keep your head from falling through ones ass, the orders read for me to report post haste to the Admiral in the Philippine, priority six, that means I fly the plane if I have to, the President of the United States is the only one who can bump me. Sounded to me like I was in a world of shit.

The orders are for military flights from the continental US to Asia (Overseas.) First problem came on the first leg from Mountain Home AFB in Mountain Home, Idaho, flight scheduled for Alaska, theses Air Force pukes weren't about to let a swabbie bump anyone, by the time I got through reaming out the Officer of the Flight Deck and the Air Police, I was sure the rest of my military time and then some would be spent behind bars. After checking my priority with the Navy things kind of settled down, I was allowed on board the aircraft, placed on a canvas seat and received a three day old lunch consisting of a cheese sandwich and a dried up pickle and a crushed orange, nothing to drink, that came later after a lot of begging, Please, Please, Please.

Pay back is hell; this aircrew had a couple of falls before we floated out of the clouds at Elmendorf AFB in Anchorage, Alaska.

Philippine's next stop, not bad on this leg of the journey, had a few high powered Navy personnel onboard, like two reserve Admirals, they didn't know who I was, but they knew I was under orders from CincPac. The Air force crew picked up on that and pretty much behaved but not before broad hints of what would happen to me if I should be seen at one of the clubs on the base upon arrival in good old PI

Entering the terminal there stands a couple of big ass Marines holding a card reading "O'Brian" how about that, my own limo service. After identifying myself, I was immediately cuffed, not without a bit of difficulty on the part of the arresting duo, driven directly to the Marine brig at Subic Bay Naval Station, after a bit of rough treatment I was slammed into a cell, I mean slammed, this is the first time I heard the word, Deserter, should I get out of this, someone is in for a major as kicking.

They had me in a cell so far removed from the main brig, it seemed like they had to pipe daylight to me. I missed dinner and breakfast the next day, you don't do this to someone who is in the habit of eating. I felt as though me stomach was trying to chew through my backbone. What ever happened to Piss and Punk, a classic Navy term of saying bread and water. At this point I'm not a happy camper, I left Idaho, a bartending job and lots of female companionship for this chicken shit treatment, someone is going to come into a world of hurt for this treatment, trust me.

Man Mountain Dean shows up on my doorstep, the other side of the bars, swinging a club that would be the envy of prehistoric man. He's big and ugly, this is the classic case of the Doctor delivering the baby, finds him so ugly, he slaps the Mother.

This Neanderthal has it in his mind that I'm a deserter from the good old US Navy and he is taking it personally to see that I see the errors of my way, translated means, he is going to stomp my ass. Error of grateful errors, he opens my cell to read to me chapter and verse out of the good book, and show me the righteous path to salvation, OK so the clown was from the hills deep in the south.

As intimidated as I am by the authority figure, I felt there comes a time to thwart abuse to my tender hide, mainly, I don't look good in black and blue.

Mr. Mountain approached me with the look in his eyes that I had one coming, about two hours later when the sergeant of the guard escorted the Major in charge of the Marine barracks and the Admirals right hand man from CincPac, the guards lunch was being eaten by yours truly and he was taking a nap on my bunk.

Attention on Deck, wow, I'm back in the military, the Sergeant of the Guard never missed a step, the Major took the situation in his stride and said, long time O'Brian, nice to see you sir, congratulations on your promotion.

The Navy Commander was somewhat putout, sailors do not go around putting down their brig guards and relaxing as though on the beach.

When the Navy ring knocker caught his breath, give him credit, he relayed a message from the Admiral, as soon as I've settled in to quarters, please report to Headquarters, this was answered in the affirmative.

From my old acquaintance the Major, I was informed, if I inflicted any permanent damage to one of his men, I'd best look forward to returning to the brig out of harms way. In a way, it was nice to be back in the saddle, these people speak my language.

At 0930 I showed up at the office for CINPAC just off the waterfront at Subic Bay, very close to the Officers Club, many a time I've received dirty looks for showing up in the bar at the "O" club, my attitude is, a drink is a drink and a bar is a bar, think I'm the only one though.

The Admiral didn't want to give his office a bad name with riffraff hanging around; he sent for me post haste. I knew he was lying when he said, nice to see you again O'Brian. Without pushing brig time I asked him, whatever happened to my medical leave and discharge, the man has always been fair and told me he ran into a lot of opposition to that plan, there were a lot of people waiting in line for me to foul up so they could further my education at Portsmouth NH making little rocks out of big ones. I had sense enough to let that line of conversation go.

According to the Admiral, Subic was becoming a hot bed of law suits against the white hat,(enlisted man), blacks assaulting whites on the base as they return to the base a bit worse for the wear and unable to defend themselves, this is the problem I want cleared up right now before we have some racial problems that will be irreversible, the Admiral layed it out without the frills.

Lighten up on the rough stuff O'Brian, don't treat everyone as a punching bag, but don't be an instigator, his next question surprised me, were you involved in the problem over on the waterfront the other night when six blacks were involved in a punch out and ended up in the Hospital. This required a flat denial on my part, but, this was just his way of letting me know he's on top of what's going on his base and the adjoining town.

Time for me to go into Olongopo, sometimes referred to as Shit City. I've been all over the world, seen quite a bit, but this place, they always managed to come up with something new, enough to make me shake my head in disbelief from time to time.

Dropping by the Marine barracks to change into civvies and haul my friend the Gunny with me, he was to be the eyes in the back of my head in town. The clerk in the OD room told me my presence was required over at the base gym, not requested, Major Chisel was waiting for me.

This is noon, everyone should be at lunch, not at the gym, didn't take long for me to get the picture, the brig guard whom I put to sleep before leaving the brig had requested a smoker (grudge boxing match) to hold up the honor of the Marine barracks. That's his prerogative, great way to solve problems that are small but could get out of proportion should they be let go.

I was met at the entrance by the Major and told to get into some trunks and prepare for a beating, this young guy that wanted a piece of my ass was about twelve years younger then yours truly, this is bullshit, I have no pride where my hide is concerned. I walked up to the ring, over to the kids corner and apologized, I ducked just in time, he tried to Sunday me, (sneak punch) that really pissed me off, I could see that this boy was going to be read to from the good book, chapter and verse.

It didn't take long for me to change into shorts and sneakers and make my way back to the ring and climb aboard. I turned to talk to the Gunny, who was acting as my second, when I received one hell of a wallop alongside the ear, no Queensberry rules here, this kid just wanted to put an end to me right now.

Before his corner crew could react, I flew out of the corner and put some serious hurt on this sneaky bastard. I was pulled off of him but only after I pummeled the hell out of him in a corner, I wasn't about to let him fall. Things settled down, we came to center ring and touched gloves, he tried to Sunday me again, I skipped away and returned to my corner to await the bell, the gunny had all he could to keep a straight face; glad he thought it was funny.

This brought back memories of when I was seventeen years old and had my first smoker in boot camp. Some black kid from Boston was using me as a punching bag, shit, his fist was in my face at will. When he said I fight like a girl my Irish came to the fore, I was being a sportsman up to this point, I lost it, as is usually the case when I'm mad, and later I was told they had to pull me off of this kid before I hurt him. This was a big mistake, I then had to learn to fight and was on the base boxing team, take one close look at this Irish kisser, I didn't get these scars picking flowers.

Back to the fight, this marine was all muscle and brawn and at this time he had one purpose in life, and that was to attend my funeral. The bell rang, he literally ran out of his corner at me, boy it's hell being loved. I faded right, dropped into a crouch and let fly a right uppercut that had him do a somersault and land face down on the canvas, something to be said for experience. I was in no hurry to visit the hospital myself. After a bit it was quite obvious that the kid was not getting up, medics were called and he was hauled off to sickbay. Major Chisel came by the locker room to tell me I didn't fight fair, yah, I know.

Leaving the base, one crosses what is known as Shit River, believe me this water, if it is in fact water, is a real dark brown, take it from me the sewerage from the town does in fact go directly into this river. Floating on this river are always a couple of barely floating boats selling everything under the sun that you could imagine and then some, I've seen a bennie boy dressed in a wedding gown awaiting his prince charming, (Benny Boy) a term used to describe transvestites.

One time just back from Nam and looking for a bit of R&R in Subic, a very nasty shoeshine boy was bugging the hell out of me on the bridge. He slapped his fingers into his black polish and slapped me across the pant leg, while still in motion he went over the rail into the water, box and all. The bonus was he splashed the hell out of the clown dressed in the bridal outfit, three locals came for me, that made my day, start it right I always say, They said, we saw that, he had it coming, and walked away. Dodged another bullet.

Two blocks from the bridge, straight down Magsaysay to #24, my home away from home, Susan Yees bar and restaurant was a welcome sight. First thing I heard upon entering the bar, where you been, you been in Subic long time. What a grape vine, the locals get the news before the base. Susan has been around Olongopo for some time, no ones sure how long, her restaurant serves good food, the bar is a service bar and doesn't encourage hanging around, her girls are high school girls who attend a local catholic school during the day, and wait table only after their home work is done. Over the bar is a cloth awning where loose change is thrown after the end of the evening, this money is collected and banked for the girls so that they may continue their education.

Topside is where the dancing girls are in the evening, Susan was known for running a no-nonsense club.

Susan has the pulse of the town, you need an answer to a question, she has it. In order to be effective in town the next few months I had to confide in Susan. She was excited to hear that some of the places would be cleaned up or closed down, and yes she would help, one had to be careful around town, the Army had their fingers in most of the pots, their Army, not ours.

I was told that my friend Colombo who had a nice club at the end of the street had sent word for me to come see him. His club was six stories tall, atrium with balconies on the inside for watching boxing, shows from Manila or just dancing. He had quite a going concern which he refused to share, he and his brother also had a club in Hawaii, and I've acted as peacekeeper on several occasions for him. He showed his appreciation by reserving a table for me each evening and telling his help my money was no good.

It wasn't long before my return that he called me to his office and said he would be selling the club; this was a real moneymaker so this announcement came as a surprise. To make a long story short, the Filipino mob outside of Manila, from the Cavite area wanted a piece of his action, it's tough to fight people that don't care whether they live or not.

Two nights later as I walked towards the club I heard firecrackers, and then recognized machine gun fire, my friend and his brother and a potential buyer were gunned down in front of the joint. Friend or no, a scene like that deserves distance before the authority's arrive, one never knows what kind of a mood they'll be in, why wait to find out, it was a good night to head for the base and get off the streets.

Shit, it doesn't rain but it pours. Arriving at the Marine barracks I found my sea bag out on the porch, what gives with that. Checking with the office orderly I found I was persona non-gratis, in other words, find another place to bunk. Seems the young marine that wanted to put me in permanent traction that afternoon was still in the hospital, shit, I didn't hit him that hard, young tough bastard like that, well screw it. I headed over to the BOQ, bachelors officers quarters, I carry an ID card from the United States Merchant Marine identifying me as an officer, Purser to be exact, I was in civvies so had no problem getting a room, merchant ships are always discharging cargo at the Navy Base.

At breakfast the next morning I sure received some hostile stares, rather then push my luck, I left before I lost my room. Officers are a funny lot; us bastards that came up through the ranks have a certain aura that's not appreciated.

Walking back towards town to do more nosing around, hell, I was given my assignment, up pulls a jeep with my former Marine Major buddy, get in you prick. Ah, romance is in the air.
We shoot up to the base hospital,

"Question Major, what's up."

"O'Brian, it must be the luck of the Irish, the kid from yesterday wants to see you, up until this point every marine on the base wanted a piece of your ass."

"So, what's happened to change their mind."

"I'll let the kid tell you."

Lying in the rack the kid looked even bigger then I remembered, he gave me kind of a half smile and embarrassed look, "O'Brian I wanted to thank you for saving my life, WOW, out of nowhere, what's with this, if we hadn't have met in the ring, and you hadn't of knocked my block off, I'd have gone on to my group as a relief in a sniper squad, since being in the hospital the Doctors have found an aneurysm that you brought to the front, I could have blacked out on patrol and been responsible for the deaths of my comrades, thanks again, and O'Brian, no hard feelings."

"None my friend, and thanks."

Leaving the hospital with the Major, he said "let's kiss and make up, you hit another one of my men and you bastard, I'll have the whole lot of the marine barracks walk over your ass."

"You sure have a way with words Major."

"You can move back into the barracks if you're of a mind to, where did you spend the night, on a cold pier I hope."

"Sorry to disappoint you, I was very comfy at the BOQ," a look of disbelief.

"You're shitting me O'Brian."

"Nope, here's my key, want to help me get my gear."

"Hell yes, just to see if you're telling me the truth."

After satisfying the Majors curiosity, and he wore out his, well I'll be damned, the Major had a couple of questions for me.

"O'Brian, the other day I had a conversation with an old friend of mine up at Sasabo, Japan, he's a Marine Captain at the disciplinary barracks there, he told me the story of a guy name of O'Brian who was Armed Forces Police there."

"So, what's your point?"

"Seems this O'Brian was a trouble shooter and, this almost floored me, a peacemaker, the story has it, that four squid (sailors) were holed up in a local hotel and were holding the maid against her will. The story is told that the local police, and the Shore Patrol were at a loss what to do and they cordoned off area and this was creating quite a scene, word came down from the Master Chief in charge of the Armed Forces Police to find O'Brian and get him on the scene. He was located at the public baths, having just gotten off of night duty. They say, he arrived at the Hotel, was met on the front steps by a Shore Patrol Chief who was told by the Master Chief not to let O'Brian into the Hotel without a club, seems he had a habit of just swinging and sorting out the facts later. The story gets better. Seems he walks down the hall on the second floor, knocks on the door, identified himself, the door was opened just a crack, wide enough for the sailor at the door to tell him to go fuck himself, that and the flash of a knife irritated O'Brian. He kicked open the door, flattened the clown at the door, walked in met another clown coming at him. This guy was given flying lessons and went sailing out and through the window; this took the fight out of the other two idiots. The room filled with the arresting Shore Patrol and the party was over, is that the truth O'Brian."

"Kind of sea storied up, but yeah, close enough."

This is where one makes the distinction between a fairy tale and a no shitter.

"That's not the end O'Brian, the story has it you had to transfer before the blacks rioted and burned you at the stake, story has it that you were pretty hard on them and took no prisoners."

"Bullshit, Major, the truth is, a large group of black sailors were responsible for some pretty mean cuts on unsuspecting white sailors and some barmaids. This was a case of just plain meanness, the umbrella with a long metal tip was what they used, the tip was either sharpened to a fine point for stabbing, or it was filed to a sharp blade, ugly cuts, they could fight all they want for all I cared. When they became vicious is when I stepped in. You're right though, I didn't have enough people to watch my back. Here in the Philippines, Olongpo outside the gate was having some serious problems, my services were requested and here I am.

I work out of the Admirals office and have pretty much of a free hand, I'm maintaining a low profile, in a few more months my tour is up and civilian life is looking better all the time."

"Horse shit O'Brian, you'll re-up, with your attitude, the civilian police will snap you up and probably treat you like a mad dog. No my friend, I think you'd best stay in the military where were used to your bullshit."

Arriving back at Marine barracks there was a message for me to report to the Admirals Office, shit, it doesn't rain it pours.

The Admiral asked me about the note I'd sent him regarding all the young sailors in the brig on legal hold, this is on people with pending legal problems and have to be kept available for adjudication by the base legal officer.

"Admiral, while in the brig here, mistakenly I might add, is when I became aware of the large number of legal holds, lot of missed movement, these are young men that were fed the old regulation bullshit in the recruiting posters, Join The Navy, See The World, a girl in every Port.

These young men leave home still wet behind the ears, nothing worldly about them, they go aboard ship, work hard to achieve upgrades in a chosen field, they arrive in Port, hit the beach, lots of girls just waiting to accommodate them and help spend their money. The old Philippine love song, I love you, no shit, buy me a drink. These young sailors get drunk, get their ash's overhauled, maybe for the first time, WOW, their in love, my thoughts on this Admiral are to put the bastards out of business."

"What business are you referring to O'Brian?"

"The thriving business of screwing over the young American sailor, first time away from home, in heat and thinking with the wrong head. The bar girl gets the sailor all hot and bothered, suggest he buy her out of the bar, usually $20.00 US, and a promise of a night of a lifetime in a local fleabag. The kicker, the desk clerk will not let us have a room if we don't have a marriage license or at least a marriage contract. This is when they make their pitch that this contract is a joke, non-binding and good for the one night, sort of a joke, Bam, his name and ship are on the phony contract.

The girl makes a beeline to the lawyer, Diogi, the local legal beagle, the Ho's best friend, and he skips on over to the Naval Base to the Legal Office and makes his claim against the lousy bastard American who took advantage of a local lovely, and now thinks he can just up and sail away. They get away with it because the legal department wants no trouble in a foreign country.

These girls have the same lawyer, and their making money hand over fist; the legal hold can be dropped for the trifling sum of $1500 US. The real down side to this is the ship is left a man short on the departing vessel; the individual is facing a court marshal for missing ship's movement.

I'd like to see these sailors get a fair shake, being young and stupid is no excuse, being taken to the cleaners by some real pros is, or at least should be."

"Why do I get the feeling that you have something in mind O'Brian."

"Well Sir, with your permission I would like to go over on the beach and read chapter and verse out of the good book to the lawyer, scumbag by the name of Diogi, Attorney at Law."

"What you propose has merit, however, I cannot condone any action that could be misconstrued by the local officials, as interference into their local customs or Criminal Justice System, we are visitors in a foreign Nation, or had you forgotten O'Brian."

"There is another matter I should like to discuss with you, this was brought to my attention only this morning. It seems that sailors returning to their ship after shore leave were set upon as they passed the park on the waterfront. It seems that a group of the sailors from the ship set up an ambush of their own, the count over in sickbay here on the base climbed considerably. Granted, the reports of any more attacks has stopped and the problem seems to have been taken care of, not to cast anyone in a bad light, this solution to the problem in discussion has all the earmarks of an O'Brian outing. If this were to be the case, this office would bring charges, since no one has come forward with charges I think we'll call the incident closed.

Please keep this office informed of the future cooperation of the lawyer you mentioned over in Olongopo, I cannot condone any illegal rough stuff, so be warned, you step over the line and your on your own, is that understood?"

"Loud and clear Admiral, may I be excused."

Next morning at the local police station in Olongopo the Chief of Police was all ears. The big question was, how to put the moneymaking lawyer out of business. My suggestion was talk to the bar girls on his payroll and threaten to pull their health card and work permit. The Chief was all for running a clean town, his off the top income didn't require any dirty tricks, the fact that the Navy could declare the City off limits to all sailors would really create problems, no business, no rack offs, increase in crime with everyone stealing from one another.

The Chief and I and three detectives made the rounds of the joints, then dropped by the lawyers office. Lots of yelling with promises of friends in high places, he was told he could have his records back when his high-powered friends in high places came around. Truth be known, if the word got out that the Base gates were going to be locked up tight do to his greed, I wouldn't give you a peso for his chances for a long life.

This is when I was told my life was not worth a plugged nickel, and I'd best get out of Town, better yet out of the Philippines. This did not bode well for a healthy future for yours truly, remember, life in this country in not held in high esteem, five bucks, US $, will see you in the ground.

Many thanks to the Chief and his Detectives, and a wise farewell, sorry to have to leave friends under these circumstances.

Next stop the Admirals Office, to make my visit to Town worth a damn, I had to convince the Admiral to convince the Base JAG Office to drop all charges against the incarcerated young sailors and let them return to duty with no further legal problems and a hell of a lot smarter.

"O'Brian you did a good job of putting a stop to the money grabbing lawyer over in Olongopo, that's one less problem we have from that side of the river."

"Thank you Admiral."

"Your enlistment is about over, what about, another month isn't it O'Brian. You can't stay here in the Philippines; we're taking the threat on your life serious. I have one more job for you. Your bags are being brought here as we speak, Major Chisel of the Marine Detachment volunteered to pack you up and drop you off at the ship at the waterfront. We had them hold off on sailing until you arrived, we had your pay records brought up to date and the vessels Disbursing Officer will see you get your monies, he's also holding your orders. You will be armed for this trip and will be in charge of a group, twelve people, this assignment will probably be the toughest you've ever undertaken, thank you for a job well-done and good luck in your future as a civilian.

O'Brian, before you leave, the Executive Officer from the ship you came to Asia on, the man keeps coming in wanting to press charges and get you court martialed for your behavior onboard while you were a ship's master at arms, specifically your treatment of the black members of the vessel."

"Admiral, this guy is the fellow that told me to eliminate the problem of blacks from bunching up in the chow line and on the mess decks, my approach was simple, I went out on the chow line on deck and said, were going to integrate, from now on, white/black in the chow line.

Later on the mess decks, the two tables smack dab in the center if the mess hall. The blacks were holding forth with all that black ass jive shit, noise, you have no idea, loud, these guys can't talk without yelling, probably comes from having such large families, they have to yell to be heard. I started moving people from the table, white, black, white black, this was not very well received. Later when this problem was brought before the Executive Officer, he denied ever having said any such thing, Bullshit, Admiral, never did I ever make these decisions without the direction of the Execs.

Usually the men on mess duty were considered screw-up, the best place to get unwanted personnel out of the division and off the job. My idea was to work their ass off, yet treat them well and fair for a job well done. My mess deck crew had a good attitude, when the Assistant Secretary of the Navy came onboard over in Southeast Asia, he complimented the crew on the shining mess deck, and this crew deserved it. It was later into the cruise that word got out that mess men were working half days, it was dinner, breakfast, next crew had lunch, dinner and cleanup, wasn't long before people were putting in for mess duty. Remember, this used to be a shit detail for the castoffs from every division on the ship, boy, did I screw up the regular theme of things.

Had an Ensign that liked to be in-charge, he gave the mess deck crew shit whenever he could. In Hong Kong while anchored out, he held my crew at attention on the quarterdeck for some silly regulation or slight to his authority, when I chased down my crew he was really holding forth with the bullshit.

I dismissed my crew, told them to finish up cleaning the mess decks then secure for the evening. This Ensign went ballistic, as far as he was concerned I was due to face a firing squad, be hung from the yardarm, wherever the hell that is, I left him standing on the quarter deck about ready to break into tears.

Did I get a write-up, you bet your sweet bippie I did, not only for insubordination to an Officer but for maintaining the filthiest mess decks in the fleet. This brought the Captain of the vessel into the picture, this accusation affected the crew, the Captain had breakfast, lunch and dinner on the mess decks and gave the galley, crew and general cleanness a 4.0.

The Ensign was told to stay off of the mess decks and was transferred upon arrival in the Philippines. I can safely say now the asshole was a wimp.

Admiral, back to my next assignment, why am I going armed?"

"O'Brian, have you heard of the most recent problem of infection from the girls in Vietnam, it's a strain that penicillin can't touch. We've got guys running around with dripping dicks and no cure, if sexually active around town they spread the disease quicker then a whore can say O.K.

The disease was injected into the Vietnamese women in order to spread the Clap or whatever you want to call it, non-specific uretheritis. The reasoning behind the whole scheme was to infect as many men as possible to keep them off of the duty roster, their care required another three or four personnel, with everyone sick or involved in health care, the fewer fighting men available to put in the field.

These men have to be isolated, and kept from spreading this curse until such time a cure is found. The solution is not a happy one; the men in question have to be isolated as I said. We have an ammo dump off of Guam that is ideal, these men will be stationed there until a cure is found or it leaves their system, fat chance of that.

These men will be listed as missing in action unless a cure is found or they die from rotting from the inside out, should that happen, we can tell the world about the miracle of survival."

"""Admiral, where do I fit into this picture?

"O'Brian, your scheduled for Long Beach, CA. You'll be discharged there. You'll be the man on the scene from the Philippines to Guam, the ship is expecting you as I said earlier, they provide the transportation, you provide the security and deliver these men to there next duty station, how simple can that be."
"Admiral, that's what scares me, it sounds too simple. "

Let me give the readers a bit of a background on VD, venereal disease. When I was first indoctrinated into Navy, besides marching all day, attending classes on firefighting, weapons, the M1 and what we classified as dirty movies, these movies showed men in the Naval Hospitals suffering from a debilitating disease, mainly syphilis. It showed the mind deteriorating, loss of motion; in short, it gave one the picture of becoming a complete idiot. As a teenager how impressive do you think that was, guess, upon being confronted with a member of the opposite sex you were supposed to run like hell the other way, or prepare yourself for the end and go with a smile on your face, how many do you think accepted the latter.

My Navy had separate urinals and shitters all painted red for the sailors with VD. Many a time I heard loud screams of pain from the infected individuals bending the plumbing while taking a leak, separate table on the mess deck, the whole nine yards, VD was considered highly infectious, this accounted for the separation from the crew.

Major Chisel drove me down to the ship tied up at the pier, she was a Military Sealift Command, Pacific vessel, an old APA. Shipping personnel, on the dock was a squad of marines, O.K. a chill ran up and down my spine, just lets say that my life flashed before my eyes, should I ask for a blind fold.

"Hey Major, what gives with the escort."

"O'Brian, you really don't know, thought you were in charge of this group transfer, seems they neglected to tell me all, I was told to pick up my orders from the ship's Captain, let's see what the hell is going on, how bad can it be, hell, he's a civilian."

From the bridge came a call, "one of you guy's O'Brian,"

"That's affirmative, are you the Captain, "
"That's right, are you coming aboard, I'm due to cast off while I still have the tide."

"Captain, I haven't seen my group yet,"

"They're on board and down below already, get the Marines onboard and lets become history around here."

"Hey, Major, are these guys part of your group."

"Yes, they are O'Brian, this was a rush for a security detail from our barracks, these guys are TAD (temporary additional duty) they'll fly back after you get to you destination. That's all I know, you'd best get aboard, their pulling in the gangway now." Thoughtless prick, I really had to hustle to get aboard.

After busting my ass to get aboard, everyone was too busy to talk to me and bring me up to date. I went looking for the group heading for Guam, finally I found them down in the center hold which had berthing and a head, this was a hangover from when these ship's were used to transport large groups of Marines to combat areas, it didn't take me long to go ballistic. These men were under armed guard, the marine on duty had his orders, can't fault the guy for that, the gunny in charge, naturally a lifer, had his orders as well. I had to see the Captain of the vessel, I'm the guy in-charge, I thought.

No sense in charging up to the bridge like a bull, like a good sailor, I asked permission to enter the bridge, that was granted, "can I speak to you Captain?"

"Not now, you O'Brian,"

"Yes Sir, I am."

"Good, when we clear the channel I'll give you a call, why don't you get squared away in your quarters in the meantime."

Not to shabby, guess they were expecting an Officer to be in charge of this detail. I was shown to a stateroom up in Officers country; lucky I didn't get a nosebleed from being up that high in the superstructure.

It felt great being underway again, and in the lap of luxury yet. We were coming up on noon and time for chow, a steward was in the passageway waiting on me to show me to the wardroom. Wrong, told him I'd make out OK in the general mess, and not to expect me in the Officers mess.

Went below to see how my group was making out, still under guard. That really pissed me off. Told the Gunny, who was in charge of the squad of Marines that the men I had on orders of transfer were not a security risk and were not to be treated as prisoners. The Gunny was easy to get along with, he was really along for the ride, on his way to Guam for a bit of R&R. He held a meeting with the rest of the Marines and all agreed, as long as no one gave anyone any shit, and followed the rules, yet to be laid down, they would be treated as transients.

The US Center for Disease Control, and the US Army Medical Research Institute for Infectious Diseases was working around the clock to curb this virus; this gave the fellows with the infection a real feeling of hope, thus their attitude.

Now is a good time to point out that the group heading for Guam knew they had a problem, had no intention of spreading their disease around, and had faith that the Navy Doctor's would come up with a cure before their beards turned white. Although clear sailing was expected, precautions were taken to prevent any of the group from swimming home, as much as I disagreed with the method, the Captain of the ship had his orders too.

Several times a day a sort of chum was thrown off of the stern by the crew of the ship, this consisted of, chicken parts, lots of blood, and fish heads and entrails, this kept the sharks on our tale and any dreamers out of the water.

Nothing was said about me eating with the crew, the Captain let me remain up in Officers country, when he found out that I was an old sailor with time in the merchant marine and had come up through the Hawse pipe and was carrying a ticket as a Purser (Officer) he gave me pretty much the run of the ship, and complete control of the transients, his passengers. The seas were glass; the weather couldn't have been nicer.

The Marine guard had an easy job of it but was still on guard, those were there orders, they gave no one a bad time and acted as expected, professionals.

The trip was smooth sailing and uneventful, after five days at sea, the ship arrived at the Ammo dump supplying the Pacific Fleet. The group I was escorting was ushered off of the vessel without fanfare; we were escorted along with the Marine Squad to the barracks where the group was to await the cure, hopefully.
What a view from the barracks, nice beach, gee dunk stand with beer, oh yeah, they had pop as well, basketball courts, playing field for baseball and other sports.

The barracks was partitioned of so that each man had his own quarters, more like a small suite, with his own T.V. Considering that these fellows were to remain isolated on this Island for God knows how long, I found no fault with them being pampered a bit.

Physical labor is out of the question, although they now looked healthy, the disease was at work in their system. The Doctors did not want to take the chance tiring out their patients and break down their immune system.

After turning over the travel orders for the group, goodbyes were said. The ship that was our transport had a few days alongside the Ammo pier to offload her Ammo before going into the yard for upkeep in Portland, OR, at Swan Island.

The Marines were taken to the Marine barracks for further orders, after being interviewed by the Islands Master at Arms, a salty Master Chief with more gold on his sleeve then you'd find at Fort Knox, I was escorted to the airstrip and helloed over to the airfield on Guam and immediately flown to San Frisco, CA, no time for a little R&R, the Navy escorted me to another aircraft heading for Long Beach, CA.

No reason was given for the bum's rush, I was overdue for discharge out of this Man's Navy, making waves, no play on words, was the farthest thing from my mind.

Although it was a Sunday, I was waltzed through the medical facility posthaste, within two hours of showing up at the Base Hospital, I was a civilian, heading back to Idaho, vowing, never to leave again.

Little did I know that my friends, Christians In Action (CIA) were responsible for the bums rush, they had plans for yours truly, they just hadn't told me yet. Doubt if the military is through with me, not knowing sure gives one an empty feeling.

ISBN 141203861-8

9 781412 038614